I0661002

James Frank Sullivan

The British working man by one who does not believe in him, and other sketches

James Frank Sullivan

The British working man by one who does not believe in him, and other sketches

ISBN/EAN: 9783741193217

Manufactured in Europe, USA, Canada, Australia, Japa

Cover: Foto ©Andreas Hilbeck / pixelio.de

Manufactured and distributed by brebook publishing software
(www.brebook.com)

James Frank Sullivan

The British working man by one who does not believe in him, and other sketches

ANNOUNCEMENT.

—•—

The Designs of Mr. Sullivan appear from week to week in the pages of "Fun." In compliance with numerous requests, a first instalment, in a collected form, is now produced under the title of "The British Working Man," which will be followed by a second collection—"The British Tradesman, and Other Sketches," including "The Complete Builder, by One who has been a Tenant." [ ].

"Fun" Office,
Fleet Street.

FUN'S BOOKS

For the Road, the River, and the Rail.

ONE SHILLING EACH,

Containing Hundreds of Comic Illustrations.

THE ESSENCE OF FUN.

THE CREAM OF FUN.

THE EXTRACT OF FUN.

INTRODUCTION.

(Evidently written by the Subjects of the Sketches, and surreptitiously inserted here when we weren't looking.)

The Party whose productions reek
  With glaring imperfections
Must be indeed possessed of "cheek,"
  To chaff in all directions!
The Party who is senseless to
  A pitch beyond endurance,
Yet sneers away, must have, we say,
  A mass of cool assurance!

The Party who believes he's done
  The loftiest of labours
In drawing wretched things in "FUN,"
  Insulting all his neighbours,—
Before he goes and sneers at those
  Absurdities which fetter
More honest folks, should mend his jokes
  And draw a little better.

And as for *fun*!—he sickens one,
  He seems so sour and cubbish!
There's not a bit of wholesome wit
  In all his comic rubbish.
The frights the wretch delights to sketch
  Are monsters of distortion!
One quite conceives the wight believes
  Their heads are in proportion!

Suppose you're told these pages hold
  Amusement or instruction,
We beg to state the error's great,
  By way of Introduction.
If folks would grace the lofty place
  Of moral lesson-setter,
Suppose the folks improve their jokes
  And draw a little better?

CONTENTS.

	PAGE
THE BRITISH WORKING MAN	1
THE BRITISH DOMESTIC	18
THE BRITISH BUMPKIN	22
THE BRITISH SIGHTSEER	24
THE BRITISH THIEF	25
"CHEMIST V. DOCTOR"	26
"DOCTOR V. CHEMIST"	27
BOAT RACE IDIOTS	28
A VISIT TO THE THEATRE	29
HOW TO LAY OUT A SUBURBAN GARDEN	30
JUSTICE IN A CORNER	32
JUSTICE AGAIN	33
ON MODELS	34
A DAY IN THE COUNTRY	36
MORE DAYS IN THE COUNTRY	37
ON TRAVELLING	38
ANOTHER RAILWAY ATROCITY	40
"NO GRATUITIES"	41
A SPECIMEN OF OUR RAILWAYS	42
THE TRIUMPH OF ROW	43
OUR WATER SUPPLY	44
OUR GAS COMPANY	45
HOT WEATHER LASSITUDE	46
THAT FELLOW CUPID	47
THE DISCONTENT OF MAN	48
THE SUPERIORITY OF "MAN"	49
THE STORY OF A GREAT MORALIST	50
SOME FELLOWS WHO ARE ALWAYS IN LUCK	51
OUR IMBECILE MAGISTRATE	52
SOME CASES REALLY DESERVING OF PITY	53
THE LAND OF GOOD TASTE	54
AMONG THE SAVAGES	55
A TRULY TERRIBLE PUNISHMENT	56
ON THE POWER OF THE HUMAN EYE	57
PRIDE IN ONE'S ANCESTORS	58
ART AND LITERATURE	59
THE ART OF RESTORING	60
THE LATEST ABORTION	61
INSTITUTIONS PECULIARLY ENGLISH	61
LA CHASSE ON LE CONTINONG	63
FALSE DELICACY	64
THE WORM THAT TURNED	65
THE ADVANTAGES OF OUR SUBURB	66
THE LIVENER-UP	67
A FEARFUL TASK	68
THE FERRY FIEND	69
THE CARRIER	70
PEOPLE WHO LOOK FOOLISH	71
THE VERY ESSENCE OF FUN	72
ON FAITH IN ADVERTISEMENTS	73
THE ONLY COURSE OPEN	74
A CRY OF DISTRESS	75
A BIT OF PRACTICAL ADVICE	76
THE PARTIALITY OF FORTUNE	77
THE MISINTERPRETED MUMMY	78
AN IRREPARABLE MISFORTUNE	79
SOME PEOPLE WHO NEVER HAVE ENOUGH	80
RAIN-WATER ON THE BRAIN	81
DISTRICT SURVEYORISM	82
THE HACKNEYED PORTION	83
MEMORIES OF A SUNDAY IN HYDE PARK	84
HOW TO "GET UP" A PETITION TO PARLIAMENT	85
THE ROUGH'S HOLIDAY	86
HOW TO LOAD A VESSEL	87
THE CUSTOM OF THE TRADE	88
THE TEMPLAR'S TRIUMPH; OR, VIRTUE ITS OWN SAFEGUARD	89
THE WAITER	90
THE BARMAID	91
AT THE BOAT RACE	92
A TALE OF AN INSULTING VALENTINE	93
THE NIGHTMARE-CATCHER	94
PAINTING FROM NATURE	95
THE MAN WITH AN IDEA	96
A DAY OUT OF TOWN	97
SOLD AGAIN—A RINKLE	98
EASTER FESTIVITIES	99
SOME SUDDEN IMPULSES PECULIAR TO CHRISTMAS	100
CHRISTMAS CHARITY	101
KING WINTER OUT OF HIS ELEMENT	102
SOME NEW YEAR'S RESOLUTIONS	103
THE DEMON SKATER; OR, ALL LEGS AND WINGS	104

THE
BRITISH WORKING MAN.

BY

ONE WHO DOES NOT BELIEVE IN HIM.

PHASE FIRST.—TIME-WORK.

"Wants a nail drove in atop o' that post? Ah! now, that's a job as 'll want a power o' thinkin' out. Ain't to be done in no 'urry, *that* ain't!"

"That 's a bit o' work as is worth getting on to. It ain't no good a dashin' at *that*!"

"Nothing like gettin' all yer tools about yer—then yer know where yer are."

"Bin at it over three year, 'ave I? Well, per see, it do want a bit o' 'andlin', But we're a-gettin' on now."

"Can't avoid kinder doin' some little damage on a job o' this sort."

"Wot! Ain't made a good job of it arter all these years, ain't I? Well, I'm a-gettin' too old for work now, so you'd better do it yerself, you 'ad."

PHASE SECOND.- PIECE-WORK.

Wants a 'ouse built? Right yer are—you leave it to me."

" No good 'angin' about and consilderin' with a job o' this sort. Git & done afore it spoils !"

" Why, 'ere's 'arf the day gone, and on'y the second storey ! Bin a-consideriu' too much !"

"Jest chuck the roof on, and there you are "

" Now then !—whatjer want a-touchin' of it afore it's dry ?"

" There now ! Wudder tell yer?"

PHASE THIRD.- CORRECTING A BUNGLE.

Enter No. 1.—No. 1 : "Leaks, do it? It ain't to be wondered at. Putty fine job he's made o' this, whoever done it ! Some folks are meddle !!

"There now—leavy we we git that to rights. Nuthin's like a thorrer workman to git things oer it."
[Exit No. 1 complacently.—Enter No. 2.

No. 2 : " Well, I am jiggered ! Leaks ? Well, somebody 'as bin a-bunglin' at this ! Lucky you called me in."

"There—that do look a bit more ship-shape. Nuthin like comin' to a good workman at once."
[Exit No. 2 satisfied. And so on.

PHASE FOURTH.—A LITTLE WORK FOR THE NEXT-COMER.

The party who does the gutters and undoes the slates.   The party who does the slates and undoes the garden.

The party who does the garden and undoes the paint.   The party who does the paint and undoes the furniture.

The foreman who says,—"Blow his soul! ought to be ashamed of 'emselves.   Letting 'em know what's what.
Disgraceful! ain't it? He'll let 'em know what's what.

PHASE FIFTH.—IDEAS OF HIS OWN ON THE SUBJECT.

"Build yer a summer-house on this 'ere lawn? Hadn't yer better 'ave a pigsty? Useful things, pigsties!"

"Mind, I don't say as I won't build yer a summer-'ouse if you're really set yer 'art on it. What I say is, pigsties is convenient."

"What! 'Ave a Swiss roof? Now you be guided by me, and 'ave a dome with a weathercock."

"What 'ave I bin a-settin' 'ere two days for? Why, I've bin a-considerin' whether we wouldn't like to make a pigsty of it after all."

"There, you are. I've built the thing so as yer can use it as a pigsty, if yer wants to."

5

PHASE SIXTH.—STRUGGLING AGAINST DIFFICULTIES.

"Well, you—p'r'aps it is just a trifle upside down—but it 'll come right after a bit."

"Not exackly wot you might say vertical—not unvertical enough to notice, though. It's all along 'o this 'ere brush."

"I mustn' ain't. So 'angin' everythink right way up with these pots brushes. Maddenin' they are!"

"Putting the paste onto the wrong side of the paper, am I? Well, it ain't to be wondered at with thisher brush—but it 'll soak through all right."

"There, it ain't no go, it ain't! A saint couldn't—couldn't 'ang it right side up with thisher 'ere 'o brushes. I declare if I ain't regler gone' orf my 'ead."

6

PHASE SEVENTH.—LIGHTENING HIS LABOUR.

POLITICAL ECONOMY (WITH THE BOY ON THE LOOK-OUT).

THE ALARM. " THE GUVNOR'S A-COMING ! "

PHASE EIGHTH.—HIS CHEEK.

"Lor' bless us, if I ain't bin and forgot the sodder! I knowed there was a summethink."

"Would yer jest stop that up with yer finger, guv'nor, while I go and get the sodder! I shaan't be moran a day or two."

"Just dropped in to see 'ow yer wos a-gettin' hon. Can't come and finish that 'ere job to-day, 'cos I 'm indisposed."

"Cold to-day, ain't it? I shall werry likely be comin' down at the end o' next week, to do that bit. I 'm orf for a skate."

"'Ere, I 've got the sodder now—but I 'as forgot my tools. Back agin soon."

"I 've just come to arsk yer if yer 'd pay me for this little job in advance, 'cos I 'm a-goin' to git married."

PHASE NINTH.—HIS NOTIONS ON GRAINING.

"Now I comes to you, and I says 'Mogginy,' I says. 'Werry well,' you says; and you combs it in, and puts twiddles with a rag. There!"

"Then I changes my mind and I says 'Oak,' I says. What do you do? Why, you up and combs it lighter and puts the twiddles t'other way."

"Then I say 'Warnut,' I says; and you makes it werry dark and turns the twiddles upsey-down! And there 's yer warnut."

"Then I up an' I says 'Marble,' I says. Then you paints it black and shies a brush at it, and there 's yer marble!"

"Wot! that like marble? You 're a disgrace to yer father, you are!"

"It 's all along o' that School Board! Where 's that there strap?"

"Well, I'm blest if 'ere ain't a chap a-doin' a proper day's work !!! We can't hn' none o' this 'ere nonsense—'tain't fair to them as wants to smoke. 'Ang his wife an' children—we ain't got no wives an' children !"

"'Ere you ! The Amalgamated Society of Working Men says as we're to 'ide all yer tools an' the one of yer 'tools behind yer, 'em solemly ain't to do no more work than nobody else. * * * Blest if he ain't a-workin' as 'ard as ever ! "

"Glad we got 'im hashed out. Now you won't do no more work than me / no' I won't do no more than you—an' we won't incourage competition, or industry, or any o' them ways."

PHASE ELEVENTH.—HIS PARTICULAR GROOVE.

"Put that round bit o' glass into that there round frame, eh! Well, yer see—I 've only bin' used to puttin' in square 'uns."

"If we could only git the whole thing square, yer see, it wouldn't be such a 'ard matter."

"There, I 've managed to make the frame a bit square."

"And I 've managed to cut the glass a bit square;"—

"And now they won't fit!"

"Oh, 'ere! I 'm off. I 've 'ad enough o' these 'ere fantastic jobs. Gimme suthin' as I bin' brought up to doin'." [Exit disgusted.

11

PHASE TWELFTH.—HIS SUFFICIENCY OF KNOWLEDGE.

"'Ere, I say, Government wants workmen to go out to Philiardelfier to pick up things. May as well go, eh? Might get a useful 'int or two?"

"Philiardelfier, indeed! Why, we've come back agin in disgust. Learn a lot there! They can't strike worth a red cent, and as to tartanin'——!"

"We don't want no teachin'. We knows 'ow to treat a non-unionist without teachin'. We're a bit more to our..... As for Phil'enteff——!"

PHASE THIRTEENTH.—HIS INTELLIGENCE.

"Why, if they ain't bin and set a INTELLIGENT feller to do MY work!"

"What's my work? Why, everythink as I 'ave a mind to turn my 'and to is my work——"

"And I'm blowed if I'm a-goin' to 'ave intelligent fellers a-doin' it. If yer don't 'and that 'ere job over to me, I'll strike."

"Ain't a-doin' it right, ain't I? Well, who said as I was? Yer no business to want such work done at all!"

"'Ere, I shall chuck up this kind o' work—(sa'y, mead, no one else can't to do it')—and take to designin' the New Coorts o' Law."

"Well, I am jiggered! If they ain't bin and set a intelligent feller to do that too!" [Strikes.

"Well, you seem to have made a good job of that, Mr. Dubber. Come and have a glass with me."

"Don't be in a hurry. Have a cigar."

"Here—take half a dozen with you

"Remarkably decent, obliging sort of fellow, that, my dear."

THE BILL.—"To drinking three glasses of beer, 1s. 6d.; to smoking one cigar, 6d.; to carriage of his duties, 1s.; to wear and tear of digestion by beer, 2s. 6d.; to society for 1 hour, 1s."

"That there's the sort o' jover as wants yer to do things for nothink, that is!"

PHASE FIFTEENTH.—ENNUI.

"'Ere's a awful place to be sent to do a day's work in! Dull? Why, there ain't no sort of amusement wotever. Nothink to okkipy yer mind and kill time."

"Ooray! 'Ere 's a dorg a-coming'. 'E 's summethink for to look at for a bit."

"There! the dorg 's gone now. S'pose I shall 'ave to take to scratching my fingers." "Oh—why, I might do a bit o' work for want ov amployment. Oh, there 's the clock a-stokin'; time to give over. I 'm off."

PHASE SIXTEENTH.—THE MASON, AND HOW TO DEAL WITH HIM.

At the New Law Courts.   Our way of sheltering the Foreign Mason from the British Mason's wrath—a rather weak-minded way, some might say !

Another way, without any weak-mindedness about it.

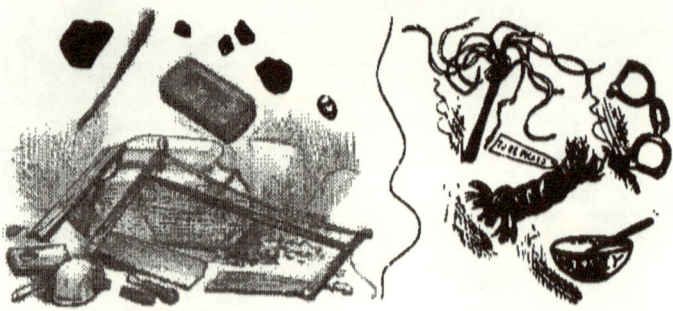

A few of the British Mason's arguments.   A few counter-arguments (highly recommended).

PHASE SEVENTEENTH.—HIS BORROWING PROCLIVITITIES. (BY A SUFFERER.)

There was a Carpentering Amateur who took great pride in his tools.

And one day he went out and left them unprotected.

And there came to the house a Workman who had been ordered to do a job.

"I say," he said to the Cook, "I've bin an' forgot to bring some o' my tools; I s'pose you ain't got any in the 'ouse to lend me?"—"Oh, yes!" said the Cook; "master's very proud of his tools—he'll be glad to lend 'em, I'm sure. I'll show you where they are."

Then the Amateur came home again, joying that he was about to rejoin his tools.

But there were some of 'em he could never, never re-join.

THE BRITISH DOMESTIC.
PHASE FIRST.—HER SCARCITY.

The Servant's Suburb.

Mrs. Wiggins, her preparations for capture.

Mrs. Wiggins, her bait.

The only "Help" for miles, her want of caution.

The same, her capture

PHASE SECOND.—HER COOKERY.

"Don't want no Cookery Books, I don't. I could tell yer all wot 's in 'em on my end."

"Don't perukwerely bile rim o' beef in a fryin'-pan, don't yer? P'r'aps yer 'll teach yer grandmother."

"Orters to roast cod-fish on a string, orters I? Didn't orter roast it at all, didn't I? Am I the cook, or ain't I? Werry well!"

"Never see sich a dirty crack as things make yer bin! My fault, is it? Oh, yus!"

"Tell yer wot it is—better get missus as does 'r same! Better do it yerself—there! I 'm orf—troubble yer for my next two years' wages—yah!"

PHASE THIRD.—HER MISFORTUNES.

" Yes, mum—dreadful destructive these things is! If this here wasue didn't sneak downstairs from the drawin'-room, when I wasn't a-noticin' and scraxpsh itself to atoms on the kitching fecker!"

" 'Ole leg of mutton in the dustole? Yes, mum—disgustin' wasteful ; but there, they 're all alike !"

" Got my best silk devess tore to bitsh the stove in Well, there—an' I never noticed it !"

" Bin' puttin' kitching-stuff in missus's new 'at ? Ohl it wasn't me as done it, mum ; and besides, I thought he'd done with it, and I 'adn't got nowheres else to put it, and 'owever was it a-come there ?"

" Reglar cubberd full of broken things ! I 'ave seen that cat a-sneaking about that cubberd—she must a-sneaked all them things from time to time, and then 'ad 'em away artful ! Worry surprisin, mum ! Yes, mum."

PHASE FOURTH.—AN INCIDENT OF FREQUENT OCCURRENCE.

PROLOGUE.—B.D. AT HOME. "Mummy—'ere's laundry! Father's brought 'ome a 'erring for dinner!"

ACT I.—IN SERVICE. "I'll just trouble yer for that little bit of brown, Cook; 'cos yer know we're got to finish that joint somehow, as missis 'ates cold meat."

ACT II.—SEEKING ANOTHER PLACE. "Well, mum, to tell the truth, I gave warning at the last place becos I couldn't get nothing to eat."

THE BRITISH BUMPKIN.

PHASE FIRST.

" Du ôi kaaa a villa carled Mossblarp ? Noa, mr o snaraoi my as oi du—
aaart 'ovelborea."

" Praaps yer saaght firt ot aaaa where down 'er :
oi be guss 'coum this waay myselt."

" No, cnara't say as we du gei maaty trovvats oat this way—
uoll 's a bit tew light fur thaat soat—we gets aaaaly wearaim an'
tuaram an' that."

" Whaa ! This be Moovblarp—be it ? Whoy, oi bea a livia;
'ere this tharty year. Way dido't yer say as tbot wor whaat
yer waaated ? oi could a tould yer then !"

THE BRITISH BUMPKIN.

PHASE SECOND.

"Nau, I ain't heard uv nobbudy hereabouts o' the name o' Jobin."

"A 'll goo an' eesk the paarson, or somebody."

"Yer ain't nare a one, are yer, heard o' nobbudy o' the neeame of Jobin, 'ev yer? Noa? Oh, well, paarson's sheuer tew knaw."

"Whoy! Paarson says as ool neeame be Jobin, And now I come to think about it, A du beeleave so it is! Well, this 'ere be a goo!"

THE BRITISH SIGHT-SEER.
HIS PECULIARITIES.

British Sight-seers awe-stricken by the remains of an ancient British village. Their credulity.

B. S.s who have climbed right up to it, and then find they haven't a pencil to write their names. Their disappointed ambition.

The B. S. who has got hold of a real prize—a genuine ancient milestone, or something. His acquisitiveness.

B. S.s attempting to distinguish the ruins of a Druidical temple from the works of Nature. Their fruitless patience.

THE BRITISH THIEF.

'THE AMOUNT OF TROUBLE HE'LL TAKE FOR NOTHING.'

Very cleverly they managed it, too! First, they went and confided in a cunning Old Gentleman who knew everything.

And he sharpened a few tools for them.

Then they carefully disguised themselves.

And lay in wait for a month or so, to find a fitting opportunity.

And at last they succeeded in snatching the coveted prize. A solid iron bell-handle, with plate and two screws of the same metal.

They were indeed rewarded. The Old Gentleman gave them the sum of one penny for the booty, and their fortunes were made.

"CHEMIST v. DOCTOR."
ONE SIDE OF THE QUESTION.

"Oh, I say, I've unfortunately swallowed half a pint of paregoric by mistake. Give me something for it—look sharp!"

"Confound it! what are you considering about? It will be all up with me in a minute."

"Well, the fact is, I daren't recommend you anything—

But these bottles are quite at your service, if you like to take your choice."

"Eh! But—look here, I'm entirely ignorant of—oh! well, here goes!"

"Dear, dear! what a very unfortunate choice! but it would never have done for me to interfere."

"DOCTOR v. CHEMIST."
THE OTHER SIDE OF THE QUESTION.

This Chemist's bliss consisted in
Inventing of a medicine;

And, oh, his mind was overrun
With joy and pride when it was done!

He manufactured, out of hand,
Enough to meet a large demand,

Resolved (when any person came
To be advised) to sell the same.

But lo! when people came to call,
They brought prescriptions, one and all;
While no one entered for the sake
Of asking "what he ought to take?"

At length to him a party went
Who'd lost his leg by accident;
The chance had come—it was enough!
That Chemist sold him all the stuff!

BOAT RACE IDIOTS.
A PROPHECY.

A party of Intelligent Young Men will choose the occasion of the University Races to make their maiden effort in boating.

They will then make their way along the river in this fashion.

And will finally (though they have the whole river to choose from) take up a position directly in the course, just as the race is approaching.

A VISIT TO THE THEATRE.
WITH ATTENDANT "CONSIDERATIONS."

"Stalls, sir?" (obsequiously) "I'll introduce you to a gentleman who'll be happy to take your coat. Of course there is no regular charge for the introduction, but," &c.

"I can recommend a lady who will look after your lady's cloaks. Of course, I, &c., some trifling consideration," &c.

"Let me make known to you this gentleman, whose programmes are unrivalled. Ahem! of course one usually, &c., some little recognition, &c., for the favour."

"Well, yes, sir; you've given me the shilling for the programme and a trifle for myself; but we generally look for some small, &c., beyond the actual," &c.

Outside.—"Well, no yer honour, I didn't exackly get yer the keb nor open the door; but I looked on, and we generally gets," &c.

HOW TO LAY OUT A SUBURBAN GARDEN.

Jones had long been looking for a nice little nook of a garden, *capable of improvement*. "And here it is," he said, "capable of any amount of improvement!" *And so it was.*

"Now to improve," he said. "First, we've got to consider how we can work surrounding objects into our scheme of beautification." And he slept upon it.

And he had enchanting dreams of the most brilliant success. First, he thought he was planting a beautiful park right up his neighbour's wall;

Then he was laying out a sweet little flower-garden on the roof of an adjacent church;

And at length he had created a perfect Paradise, extending over as many acres as you please.

HOW TO CONSTRUCT A "ROCKERY" CHEAPLY AND EFFECTIVELY.

One of Jones's Chimneypots.

A few of Smith's Tiles.

Some of Brown's Bricks.   And so on.

JUSTICE IN A CORNER.

"Better adulterated? Well, it's no good coming to the poor retailer about it. Try the agent."

"Oh, don't come upon me. I'm only the agent. Go to the wholesale man."

"Adulterated! Master don't know nothing about it. 'E's only the wholesale man. You tax the grower with it, over in Brittany."

"Butter! I haven't anything to do with it. Ask the cow."

"Don't ask us! Cows haven't anything to do with butter."

So that Justice threw away his sword and scales, and gave the matter up.

JUSTICE AGAIN

Since Justice had suffered such difficulties over the adulteration affair, he 'd been casting about for a fresh object ;

When he perceived an unruly crowd going somewhere.

Here was the subject ! "Disorderly Houses!" This is Justice's notion of a Disorderly House. So he set to work.

In the meanwhile, why doesn't somebody take in hand Justice's own Disorderly House?

And Justice might go for a change of air during the time

ON MODELS.
THE AMATEUR MODEL.

"I want you to stand for me. It won't hurt you in the least."

"I should like you to put an expression of sorrow in your countenance, as if all were lost."

"Just wave your hand so, as if waving an adieu. Yes—that's beautiful— only I'm afraid there's a certain want of freedom in the attitude."

"You won't mind my saying it—but there's a sort of—so to speak—merriment in your expression, incompatible with despair, as it were."

"Will you leave off grinning?"

"That will do for to-day. When I want you again I'll cut my he——I mean to say, I'll let you know."

THE PROFESSIONAL MODEL.

"Want me to stand like so, Mum, with my 'and on
my breast?"

"I see what you want. You want 'Misery.' Like so, Mum;
'and on breast, mouth drawn down, eles 'and I say, as if
'spoken."

"Not 'Misery'? Then it's 'Meditation' you require—
that 's doin in this way."

"Not 'Meditation' neither? Then it's 'Supplication.' No! There's
no other pose with the 'and on the breast, you know!"

A DAY IN THE COUNTRY.

"Ah, my boy! I'll take you round the place after breakfast. You cockneys *do* get a chance of a breath o' fresh air when you come into the country!"

"Now 'ere's the ditch that carries off the waste from Perkwater's Steam Mills, twenty mile up."

"And 'ere's the pigs."

"And 'ere's some o' the best land you'll see for miles. Just been putting down some fish manure."

"What! Off to town a'ready? Well, if you won't stay and have another breath o' fresh air——"

MORE DAYS IN THE COUNTRY.

"Going on a walking tour? Tell yer what, my lads, you go to my county—good living there! Talk about plenty! Plenty to eat there, I can tell you."

Say in Devonshire, for instance. "Clotted cream, Sir! Oh, I know what you mean—we had a bit down from London last year as a present."

At the Seaside. "Fish, yer honours—oh, ah, yes! Oh, I dessay you'll get a bit when the train comes in from London."

Among the pastures. "Well, no, we don't have much milk to spare, bacos it goes up to London, you see; but I might get you half a glass."

And so we hurried back to town to get something to eat.

ON TRAVELLING.
SOME RAILWAY "ATROCITIES."

Two minutes to catch the train : Study of a "Queue" waiting while a Blaséd Dame wavers for ten minutes as to whether she shall pay in a threepenny piece or three pennies.

The Sweet Lady who gets into a smoking carriage and complains that smoke always makes her cough.

The Genial Old Gentleman who prefers to leave the booking-hole the wrong way.

SOME MORE RAILWAY "ATROCITIES."

The Gentleman whose "time is money," and who "summonses" the
Company when the train is two minutes late.

The Gentlemen who must have something to do when they travel.

The Gentleman who never can find room in the class (3rd) for
which he holds a ticket.

"Gracious, sir! travellers have no consideration for anybody
but themselves!"

The —— [ahem !] who can't make room for a lady.

ANOTHER RAILWAY ATROCITY.
THE COUPLE-CATCHER.

A newly-married couple on a tour, and the Catcher with her eye on 'em

The Catcher on the scent.   Plans for eluding the Catcher.

Collapse of the plans. The subsequent journey.

"NO GRATUITIES."
A TALE OF A RAILWAY.

"Want your ticket, Mum? Hush! Trust to us and there will be no difficulty. We'll manage it for you."

I'll get your ticket for you and he'll look after your traps. They persist in their corporate mission, and refuse gratuities.

"You want to go by train, Mum? Confide entirely in me. I will find you a carriage at whatever cost. Remember I did it."
[He effects the unprecedented move, and refuses a gratuity.

"Very clever of my friend to find you a nice carriage, Mum. You shall continue in it—I can do this for you, and will."
[He refuses a gratuity.

A SPECIMEN OF OUR RAILWAYS
FROM RECENT REVELATIONS.

Departure of a Rash Passenger.

The Passenger on the Journey.

A sketch from the carriage window on the way. Station Master (aged thirteen) and Telegraph Clerk (aged eleven) doing their duty.

The Signalman.

THE TRIUMPH OF ROW.

BY OUR DISGUSTED HERMIT NOW VISITING TOWN.

OUR WATER SUPPLY.

"Jane, this water is not at all clear. I can see living organisms in it with the naked eye. Go up and see if there's anything in the cistern."

And that unhappy Jane went up.

"John, my boy, it's very strange that Jane does not return from the cistern! Go up and see if there's anything the matter."

And the ill-starred John went up.

"It is very extraordinary! Neither the house-maid nor my son has returned! I will go myself and see!"

And he went up; and a living organism, which had glutted the careful attention of the Water Company .....

"Gas is very bad this evening.

" I 'll just get a light and see where the flame is."

" Where the deuce is the burner?"

I say, Mr. Gas Company, your gas is very bad—just keep in and see, ..." illuminating power of fourteen candles," murmured the Company to itself as it stepped in,

" Why, you 've got the candles alight—it says nothing about 'fourteen lighted candles,'" said the Company.

" Blow 'em out. Now, then, the gas beats em hollow ! "

HOT WEATHER LASSITUDE.

"Want to look at a few diamond rings and things? Oh, all right—you'll find 'em in window."

"All serene - bother the tickets—put 'em down somewhere—I'll trust yer all."   "Oh, there! confound the thing! I won't pick it up."

"Q-o-oh! I say! What's to be done? The corks aren't drawn!"

THAT FELLOW CUPID.

"Bless me!" said Cupid—(for it was the nineteenth century, and he wasn't as young as he *had* been,)—"My word! To think I could ever have gone about like that Disgraceful!"

And wherever he eyed he came across portraits of his younger self in that steamy attire. "That's him was used to dress like us!" said vulgar boys.

And the ladies stared at him and sniggered until he blushed up to the eyes.

THE DISCONTENT OF MAN.

"I say, Brown," said Jones, "let's have a real, good, old-fashioned Christmas." "Oh, yes!" said Brown; "where's your snow and all that?"

But Jones soon made provision for that sort of thing:

And with the help of a little artifice and the permission of the Squire, he soon made our village look seasonable.

"Now," said Jones, "let's sit over the fire and pretend to shiver."

THE SUPERIORITY OF "MAN."

"It's on'y Bill's ole woman. He've bin a-bising her a bit, and he knocked the top of 'er 'ead off, and she 'ed to 'ave it put on agin."

"Oh! it ain't nothink. On'y two pennies' 'eads as that Bill 'as amputated, and that there dorg of 'is as 'e 'as a-experimentin' on."

"Wy am I a-weepin'? Wy, 'ere 's a pore creetur 'as bin an' fell down and put a finger out o' jint! Oh, yer needn't grin! It ain a woman nor a phenomenon nor a dorg—it 's a man now—it 's pore Bill 'isself!"

THE STORY OF A GREAT MORALIST.

This is a young man who wrote a novel for lucre. Lest as to interesting it to convey any moral whatever, why, bless your heart, he didn't.

And this is a Critic who read it, and said, "Dear me! this story contains a beautiful moral lesson—it should be read by the young and perused by the aged."

And this is Mr. Grundy, who presented the book to his daughters to read.

And this is the surprise of the Author on hearing that his story taught a beautiful and instructive lesson.

And this is the Rev. Bishop who yearned to grasp the hand of the greatest social teacher of the age.

And this is the Lady who was so touched by the book that she bought up all the remaining copies, to send to the aborigines.

And this is the Author's brutal and overbearing vanity on finding he was a great moralist.

And this is the moral of *this* story,—that your Critic is your only moralist.

SOME FELLOWS WHO ARE ALWAYS IN LUCK.

"I'm a-going your way, mister, so I'll shew yer the road."   "Prime snuff, ain't it? I'll give you a dose."

"Nice good fellows, those three! You must know 'em! I'll bring 'em down to stay at your place for a week."

"I know you want a good spin. There!——I'll introduce you to my wife!"

OUR IMBECILE MAGISTRATE.

"What dreadful atrocities they commit
in the East!" said our own Imbecile
Magistrate.

That day there was brought to him a culprit
who had impeded traffic with a top;

And our I. M.'s wrath was let loose
against the miscreant to the extent of
seven years and the cat.

Then our I. M. dined,

And his wrath abated;

So that when another culprit was brought
who had skinned a horse alive,—

Our I. M. felt amiable, and fined him one shilling, dismissing him
without a stain, &c.

"Why, these Eastern atrocities get more atrocious every
day!" he said next morning. The fact was, he was reading
about his own doings of the day before, only he was slightly
worse this morning, and didn't recognise his own name.

SOME CASES REALLY DESERVING OF PITY.

"There! all the time I've been out, if that no-mind hasn't been givin' full weight to all the customers!"

The Carrier. "This is a nice sort o' world. I 've carried fifty parcels this 'ere blessed day, and not a single one of 'em has bin paid for twice over!"

"Injoyed my 'oliday? No, I ain't! Why, I 'aven't bin thoroughly drunk nor for so much as 'arf a hour all day!"

THE LAND OF GOOD TASTE.

There's a land where the people go trooping in packs
To smirk at a murderer's image in wax,

While the wretched original, still in the gloom
Of his prison, in agony waits for his doom.

There's a land where a person who's tried for a crime
And acquitted as guiltless, in process of time

Stands a capital chance of sustaining the blow
Of observing his figure in wax at a show.

There's a land where the crimes which you shame to recite
Form the topic of converse among the polite,

And the table discussion of every one;
And the greater the horrors, the greater the fun.

AMONG THE SAVAGES.

LANDING. The first experience of them.

IN THE INTERIOR. Reception of Foreigners.

IN THE INTERIOR. Preparations for wife-roasting by a native Cannibal.

A TRULY TERRIBLE PUNISHMENT.

PROLOGUE :—The Rough out of Jail.—Dirt, discomfort, and rent to pay.

Dinner-time.

ACT I. The Crime.

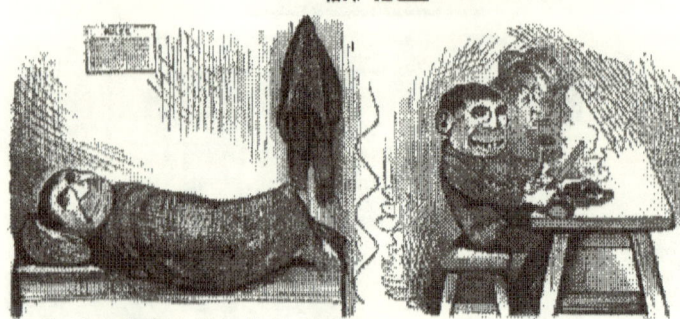

ACT II. A Terrible Punishment. The Rough in Jail :—Cleanliness,
comfort, and no rent to pay.

Moral :—Criminality is the Best Policy.

ON THE POWER OF THE HUMAN EYE.

"Why, this umbrella's a complete swindle! I'll go to that shop and I'll break every bone in their backs!"

The Determined Entry.

The Attitude of Impending Wrath.

The Defiant Eye—its Effect.

Its Further Effect.

The Swaggerer's Collapse.

PRIDE IN ONE'S ANCESTORS.

"There! *Your* grandfather never wore a stock as big as *that!* Yar!"

"I assure you *my* father used to correct me like this."

"My great-aunt was universally *admitted* to be the ugliest woman in Bath."

"Beshrew me! It isn't every man whose ancestors used to cut off folks' ears! *Mine* used. Here 's one."

"Now, sir, that 's my great-grandfather's wooden leg. It 's what I call a Wooden Leg, sir. They knew how to make wooden legs in those days, sir!"

ART AND LITERATURE.

There was a Comic Artist who drew a caricature of a public man ;   Who was so delighted with it that he took the Artist under his patronage.

And the Successful Artist attained such a position that he had to brush his hair and order a dress suit.   Encouraged by the Comic Artist's immense success, a Comic Writer went home and wrote a little satire about the public man ;

When, lo ! *this is the reward he got !*   "Sir !" said the satirised one, "why, he actually *hinted* that I was a *Pig !*"

THE ART OF RESTORING.

The Original Designer (some few hundred years ago):—"There— that's my idea of the thing—something quite plain and simple." (He passes away, together with the few hundred years.)

The Modern Architect:—"Grand ruin, isn't it? Not enough to restore from? Bless you! I've restored a whole cathedral from a chip of pavement."

"There now, that's about the thing the Original Designer evidently intended—something florid and complicated."

"All you have to do, you know, is to get yourself thoroughly imbued with the *spirit* of the Original Designer."

Spirit of the Original Designer, taking a look round:—"Well, what strange things these modern *do* design, to be sure. Quite original, though!"

THE LATEST ABORTION.

Fun had long been pondering over the two means of making his fortune, when he suddenly hit it !——Pander to the prevailing taste for the unnatural and the revolting.

He would procure the most startling specimen of deformity.

So he lay in wait, and spotted his specimen going in to see the Pig-faced Lady.

He came up with him, engaged in gazing admiringly at the "Japanese Gemini, or the Twisted Twins;"

And captured him in the act of gloating over the Living Skeleton.——And he now has him daily on view as the BIGGEST ABORTION OF THE AGE—the Man with a Distorted Mind ! But the thing failed, for the "Curiosity" was voted quite common, after all !

The Umbrella Charge. A crowd hurrying *to* its train meets a crowd hurrying *from* its train. By the ingenuity of the Railway Company, there's only one gate for the two crowds. In the course of two hours or so both crowds will have struggled through, much damaged.

A Gathering Storm. Taking up the pavements in the busiest part of the year.

Common Preservation. Sketch of the prettiest corner of Barnes Common, 1877.

LA CHASSE ON LE CONTINONG.

BY OUR OWN COMMISSIONER, WHO CAN'T BEAR TO WRITE IN ONE LANGUAGE.

FALSE DELICACY.

This is a gentleman who thirsts for a pair of one-and-sixpenny gloves, but doesn't like to ask for them, because it looks mean.

So he goes in and asks to have a look at some little thing not over a thousand pounds.

And he doesn't much care for any of these, but he'd like to have a look at those things in that box up at the top there.

No-o-o, he doesn't care for any of those things either.

So he says, in a casual way, he supposes they haven't anything in the way of—that is, in the nature of—you know—say a pair of gloves at about eighteenpence, or one-and-sixpence, or so? Oh, yes, they have.

"By Jove!" he says, as he goes along, "wonder whether the feller 'ud change 'em?" And the feller actually won't—so he loses that gentleman's custom.

THE WORM THAT TURNED.

Departure of a Good-tempered Citizen for town.

The Edge-of-the-pavement-water-cart Torture.

The Dust Torture (under the patronage of the Parish Authorities).

The Wind Torture.

THE ADVANTAGES OF OUR SUBURB.

"What I like about a residence in the Suburbs is the walks you can get, you know!"

"Now, here's a spot where you won't meet a soul for weeks together." ("I don't blame the souls I muttered Jones.)

"Positively won't go a step farther, eh? Then let's have a pipe, and stay here till it dries up a bit."

THE LIVENER-UP.

"We shall be charmingly livened-up presently. I have asked Mr. Brown, the well-known comic artist, to come. He's sure to be *so* entertaining!"

Looking out for the Livener-up.   The arrival of the Livener-up.   Intense interest of the About-to-be-livened-up.

The Livener-up himself.   General Collapse.

A FEARFUL TASK.

There was a Leader-Writer on a daily paper who, about *February*, begun to waste with care and turn from his food.

As March approached, his nights became restless and burdened with uneasy nightmares.

And at the beginning of that month folks on the Putney tow-path began to be alarmed with the sight of an agonised figure stalking up and down.

Whenever the Leader-Writer heard a knock at his door, he started wildly from his chair.

At length the dreaded summons came. "Jellattop," said the Editor, "you must write me an *entirely new* article about the Boat-Race—something never written before." *The blow had fallen!*

THE FERRY FIEND.

AS SEEN EACH YEAR AT THE BOAT RACE.

The Ferry Fiend conjures his victim to embark.

He lands them on an island whence escape is impossible.

THE CARRIER.

"This shall reach its destination to-night, sir," said the Carrier; "I swear it!"

And he put it carefully aside to await the departure of the cart.

Meanwhile a Young Couple waited for the arrival of their wedding-cake, to be returned.

And slowly that parcel glided from youth to prime, from prime to superannuation, where it had been put down to await the cart.

And still the Couple sat, waiting. . . . .

It was late in the next century that a Carrier delivered the remains of what had once been a parcel containing a cake. "They'd most every note with that parcel 'cos it were important," he said.

PEOPLE WHO LOOK FOOLISH.

The Young Man picked out by the Purse-Trick Gentleman and requested to examine the article.

The Youth requested to tell us all that delightful story about that little affair, because he does tell it so well!

The Sight-seer fixed by the eye of him who "Shows the place," and singled out as the victim of his explanation.

THE VERY ESSENCE OF FUN;
OR, THE FATE OF FUNNY INCIDENTS.

There was a poor, broken-hearted Funny Incident called on us the other day, and this was its sad history:—

"I occurred" (it said sadly) "in real life; and I was so funny that people positively roared over me,

"And retailed me to one another in frantic mirth.

"But a clever Journalist got to hear o' me, and made me into a whole column to increase my humorous, and people read me so; and they smiled faintly!

"Then a talented novelist saw me, and exclaimed, 'A splendid idea for a comic novel—I'll make it funnier still!' And people read the novel; and they thought it was meant to be serious!

"And at last a great Burlesque Writer found me, and said, 'What a funny notion for my burlesque; I'll make it funnier than ever!' And people saw the burlesque, and wept at me—for they thought I was a tragedy!!"

And with these sad words the poor Funny Incident prematurely expired.

ON FAITH IN ADVERTISEMENTS.

"Here! By Jove, my love; here's just what we've been looking for so long. 'Pleasant Detached Villa, in thorough repair, with magnificent view, and close to a lake!'"

So they bought the place at once, and then went off joyfully to look at it.

The Villa.

The View.

The Lake. And from that day they became prematurely old.

THE ONLY COURSE OPEN.

"Fine bit of sketch, that!" said our Sketcher.   "Grand—so   "Ha! A Foe!"
magnificently diiophidated!"

"Yes!!!"   The only course.

The friendly overtures.   The Sketcher at peace.

A CRY OF DISTRESS.

There's a man who always pounces upon our Comic Artist whenever he sees him,

And will take his arm and say, "I say, why don't you do some comic drawing about my adventure with a mouse!"—(or a jug, or something)—" Capital subject for you!"

And then he makes our C. A. sit down while he repeats his entirely personal and uninteresting adventure.

"There!" he exclaims. "There 'an idea!" And he always stands on our C. A.'s coat-tails until our C. A. swears to use the idea. Our C. A. has already perjured himself fifteen times. What is to be done?

A BIT OF PRACTICAL ADVICE.

When you make an appointment to meet a friend, never fix upon a long, straight piece of road as the meeting-place. If you do, you catch sight of your friend a long way off, and embarrassedly pretend not to see him, to avoid commencing your smile of greeting too soon.

Then, arriving, say at that post, you suddenly burst into a ghastly unnatural grin, which you have been preparing for a hundred yards.

Still, you find you have begun too soon, and you grin like two idiots, and over after despise one another!

Whereas, had you fixed on a corner, you would have come upon one another suddenly, burst into a great, glad, intelligent smile of welcome, and conceived a mutual attachment never to fade.

THE PARTIALITY OF FORTUNE.

It was a row where humble folks
Were made by cleaning window-panes
Their precarious daily bread—
Completely humbugged—by

One opposite who scratched his head,
And smoked, and gazed about the sky
Whereon that window-cleaner swore
That he would window clean no more.

"I am resolved," I heard him say,
"To take the lodging opposite,
And scratch, and smoke, and gaze all day—
The work is very nice an' light!"

He knew not, in his want of guile,
The Scratching Smoker was a Bard;
He little thought that all the while
He gazed, he was a-thinkin' hard.

The Bard became so wealthy that
Within a month, or two, or three,
He could afford a chimney hat,
And even wished for his tea.

The cleaner smoked at quite a rate,
But his success refused to come—
Which only shows how Mrs. Fate
Makes shameful favourites of some!

Things got so bad that (hapless wight!)
The "Home" became his end resort;
While Mister Fate—serve him right!—
Was forced to pay for his support.

THE MISINTERPRETED MUMMY.

It was an Ancient—one who had
  Descended from Egyptian stocks;
And he conceived a sudden fad
  To paint his pet tobacco-box.

A cat, an eye, a pig, a bird,
  He'd cut, and fill 'em up with paint.
His little ones were most absurd—
  The whole effect was very quaint!

He knew no more of lines of kings
  (The mighty Isis' self forbid !)—
Or any such historic things
  Than Kob (the Sacred Beetle) did.

The gods forbid it, seeing to
  The priesthood he did not belong,
And any paltry layman who
  Knew any blessed thing did wrong.

He merely went and chiselled at,
  And coloured in, each queer device
Because he had a notion that
  The thing would look extremely nice.

And when he'd viewed his work with pride,
  And found it suited to his ends,
He curled him neatly up and died,
  And then was pickled by his friends.

In modern ages, in that land
  There came a-wandering about
A scientific person, and
  He found the box and dug it out.

He was a party who could boast
  A very keen and subtle wit;
And very soon he'd made a most
  Important story out of it !

At first the Ancient felt a sting,
  And thought that "chaff" might be designed;
But as they made him out a king,
  He grew contented in his mind.

78

AN IRREPARABLE MISFORTUNE.

"'Ere—Mister—sir—your little boy's bin an' trod on my pipe, and I 've got a wife and family, and I 'am a 'ard-workin' man, and I 'm ruined, I am ! That there pipe was worth more 'n a 'underd pound to me !"

"'Arf a crown maky me ! Well—yes—that 'll do. Thankee, sir !"   "Wot's he sprung, Bill ?"

Scene next morning. Waiting for the pipe-smasher.

SOME PEOPLE WHO NEVER HAVE ENOUGH.

" Will you tell the gentlemen, miss, as we 've took the casks in, and we wouldn't mind a drop o' beer ? "

" Well—Chucey   blackeyes !   I wants yer to !   I 'd like one—Now then ! "

" What I say is—Give me a pipe and a glass."

" I want to see one or two cravats. "

RAIN-WATER ON THE BRAIN.

A melancholy person, with an aspect as of blight,
Was straying very sadly, and his coat was buttoned tight.

Oh, drinking very deeply had he been from sorrow's cup,
And dismally he grumbled at his "gingham" (which was up).

He wandered over Africa, Siberia, and Spain,
Believing that it did (although, of course, it didn't) rain.
The pitying inhabitants discovered that his brains
Were softened by a residence in England (where it rains).

He wandered on (his sad delusion clinging to him yet),
To find a happy haven where the weather wasn't wet.
He wandered on (believing that it rained in every spot),
And reached the large Sahara (where the sun is rather hot).

But he muttered, "Well, I never!" and he murmured, "I declare!"
(Fallaciously believing it was raining even there!)

And when I last perceived him in the Desert, he had lit
(Or lighted) up a bonfire—just to dry himself a bit.

DISTRICT SURVEYORISMS.

"I'll tell yer what, Jack; if it wasn't as the District Surveyor 'ad said it was all right, I'd a'most say as them railoman down there wasn't enough to support this 'ere 'ouse."

A District Surveyor in the act of failing to detect any particular bulge in the wall.

"Upon my word, Brown, if it were not for the reassuring activity of District Surveyors, I should really be afraid to stand near some of the houses they build now!"

THE HACKNEYED PORTION,
AN EPISODE OF AN EATING-HOUSE.

"What have you to eat, Waiter? 'Jugged hare—roast goose—veal cutlet, eh?' Let us have some jugged hare."

"Waiter, this not like jugged hare. Take it away, and let's have some roast goose."

"Why—Waiter, this roast goose is the jugged hare turned upside down. Here, give me a veal cutlet instead."

"Why, here—this veal cutlet is the roast goose, with tomato sauce over it!"

"I'll go and dine somewhere else—I'll——"

Then a meek young gentleman enters and asks for turkey and sausages—and he didn't like to say that jugged-roast-hare-goose-cutlet wasn't like turkey—so that portion was got rid of at last.

"Six millions, indeed ! We have men here to prevent the pockets of the taxpayers being picked !"   A "peace-at-any-price" party.

An Argument on our War Supplies :—" It ain't meaning we 're wastin' fur, not provisions. It 's men to eat 'em ! We 've got no men to eat 'em !"

"And, after all, what 's six millions ! Why, the merest trifle !"

HOW TO "GET UP" A PETITION TO PARLIAMENT.

SEE RECENT REMARKS OF THE PARLIAMENTARY COMMITTEE.

It was absolutely necessary that our Petition about the Pump should be signed by 10,000 resident working men; but this was difficult to manage. In fact, the whole population of our parish is given in the sketch above.

However, with the aid of our invaluable parishioner, Tim, who could sign to no end of different hands,

And of the scholars who came from the next parish to Master Tattson's school,

And of two friends of our Bob, who could never sign their names twice in the same way,

And of other providential circumstances, we managed to work up the petition to the requisite sum—and far—what's to said out if we have slipped on an extra name or two?

THE ROUGH'S HOLIDAY.

ITS PECULIARITY.

" Got a 'oliday to-day? So 've I." (*With a sudden inspiration*)
" Let 's buy a couple o' sticks, to begin with."

" 'Ere 's a putty place, ain't it ?" (*Enthusiastically*) " Let 's
knock the flowers 'orf !"

" Well, we ain't done a bad 'oliday, 'ave we ? We 've broke lots o' trees an' 'edges, and spiled a kewby garding, an' trampled down some
roses an' thungs, an' 'eaved all the lates about 'ere. Now let 's set fire to a 'Common, an' go 'ome to supper."

HOW TO LOAD A VESSEL.
(EXTRACTS FROM THE LOG OF THE "SETTLER.")

"Pr'aps we ain't got over-much room to move; but it 'll be all square, my lads, so long as we don't get any storms, nor any lee-shores, nor any accidents."

It 's unfort'nit we 're packed so tight, my lads. Might ha' saved them masts if we could ha' got to the tools!"

"Precious lucky it was a soft lee-shore, ain't it? We 'll have to stick here till the mutton come an' move a box or two. Couldn't turn your head and see if the others have been washed overboard, could yer?"

"Might get another couple o' chests stowed on the truck," said the Captain, "and then get out to sea at once."

87

THE CUSTOM OF THE TRADE.

"This dinner-set for seven pounds"
(The Customer observed) "is cheap
Beyond my expectation's bounds!"
But oh! he wasn't very deep.

But when the service home they brought,
According to his stated wish,
That party looked in vain for aught
Beyond a solitary dish.

"I'll back that dinner-set to top
All others I have ever seen,"
He said, returning to the shop;
"But you forget the soup-tureen."

"No service that you've ever seen,"
The Shopman said, "I beg to state
Included any soup-tureen—
But you can have it separate."

"That dinner-set is very nice,"
The Buyer said, "upon my soul—
And singularly cheap in price—
But you forgot the salad-bowl."

"A salad-bowl," the man explained;
"It is a thing I never knew
That any dinner-set contained—
But we can get it made for you."

The Buyer said, "That art of ours
Is such as no one hesitates
To qualify as very fine—
But you've omitted all the plates."

Replied the Shopman, "As to plates,
They've basins; you can 'ave 'em ample—
The Custom of the Trade dictates." * * *
It knows a thing or two, the Trade!

THE TEMPLAR'S TRIUMPH; OR, VIRTUE ITS OWN
SAFEGUARD.

"He's a G. T.," said three birchings (suborned by us for the purpose) ;
"let 's make him tight !"

So they went and procured

Some intoxicating liquors ;

Mounted by unprincipled and irregular means to his second floor * * *

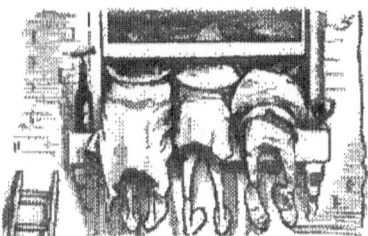

And gazed, crestfallen, through the window.

For the Good Templar had anticipated them in their full design, and they were baffled.

THE WAITER.
OR, THE WAY OF ALL MEN.

(No customers inside.) "Pray—oh, pray!—step in and take some refreshment, your Grace! I implore!"

(One customer inside.) "Will your honour condescend to step within and dine?"

(Three customers inside.) "Dinner, sir? yessir! walk in, please."

(A good sprinkling of customers inside.) "That way in. Daresay you'll find a seat somewhere."

(Crowded.) "What! Want to dine! Well, of all the impidence I ever——! You be off, or I'll give you in charge—d'year!"

90

THE BARMAID.

8 A.M.—A few things to clean up.

ANY TIME IN THE DAY.—The Young Man of enlightening conversation.

DITTO.—The Lady who mutters about a "forward minx."

5.15 P.M.—The Workman (knocked off for the day) who says, "Ah! she 'as a nice easy time of it, she do!" And goes off to his "convivial."

12.30 P.M.—The Amiable Gentleman who talks about reporting her for daring to be sleepy.

AT THE BOAT RACE.

ON THE ART OF IMPROVING THE OCCASION.

How to obtain wealth.

How to obtain experience.

How to display one's reckless courage.

How to impress with one's technical knowledge.

How to finish the day.

A TALE OF AN INSULTING VALENTINE.

Brown saw a libellous Valentine representing a prize pig, that man is, to be sure!" A few minutes later Jones saw it. and ask for it, so he stared undecidedly every day;

"By Jove!" he chuckled, "I should like to post that to Jones—how absurdly fat "I've half a mind to send that to Brown!" But it seemed undignified to go in

While Brown's was a perfect mass of doubt, longing, and vacillation. But at length they both screwed up their resolution, arrived at the same moment, and rushed into the shop, where they were so embarrassed at each other's presence that they couldn't say a word.

"They'd just stept in—a—to get that Valentine to—to send to—to Robinson!" they said, with a sudden lucky thought and a sigh of relief. "How any man can be so ridiculously rotund as that Robinson——" they said.

And when Robinson received it he grinned, and said, "By Jingo! this'll do for that landlady of mine. To think of any woman's attaining such an outrageous degree of corpulence——" And he nearly died of laughing over the recollection.

THE NIGHTMARE-CATCHER.

One Christmas Eve a Travelling Showman consumed a hearty supper of under-done pork

Yet, as he retired, a certain mystery of manner showed that appetite alone had scarce dictated the course.

And observation through the keyhole proved that the Showman revolved certain schemes.

He was observed to place his nightcap on a bolster,

To smash in the head of his drum,

And then, retiring to a dark corner, to wait.

That same night, the weird form of a Nightmare was seen going its rounds.

Attracted by the odour of pork, still traceable in the air, it stood before the Showman's caravan;

And entered, to seek its victim.

PAINTING FROM NATURE.

AN ESSAY ON THE BENEFITS OF BODILY REFRESHMENT.

DISSATISFACTION.   DESPAIR.

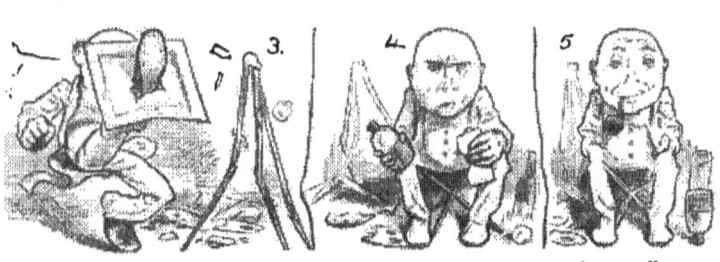

DISGUST.   LUNCH.   RETURNING HOPE.

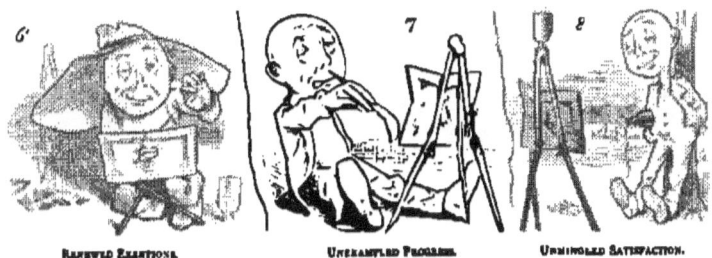

RENEWED EXERTIONS.   UNEXAMPLED PROGRESS.   UNMINGLED SATISFACTION.

THE MAN WITH AN IDEA.

A Newspaper Reporter, once on a time, suddenly thought of something quite original to say in his next description of Lord Mayor's Day.

Of course every Editor was anxious to get possession of him, body and soul,

And sent his wife and daughters to wheedle his idea out of him.

Nay, even went so far as to cast specially imposing type wherewith to set up his copy.

The fish arrived, and his minions swarmed with devim hanging at his elbow.

But glory had departed, and all was a blank. The miserable man didn't open that door, for he had forgotten his idea.

And we fancy this is often the case with many other clever folks—including ourselves.

A DAY OUT OF TOWN.

ONE OF OUR NATIONAL CHARACTERISTICS.

Before the Start. Putting up some snacks for the journey.

At the Railway Station. Using up some of the snacks.

On the Beach. English ideas of complete enjoyment.

SOLD AGAIN—A RINKLE.

Just at the beginning of November Jack Frost got up with mischief in his eye.

"Here 's a party going to skate!" he said. "I 'll just freeze him to the marrow, and delude him with the anticipation of a real good winter."

"I 'll freeze the top of the water just enough, with my cold bellows, to let him get on;

"And then I 'll thaw it all at once with the warm 'uns, and he 'll tumble in!" But somehow that ice wouldn't melt. "Why, there 's something wrong with water!" said Jack Frost, in a great fright.

EASTER FESTIVITIES.

BY OUR SIGHTSEER.

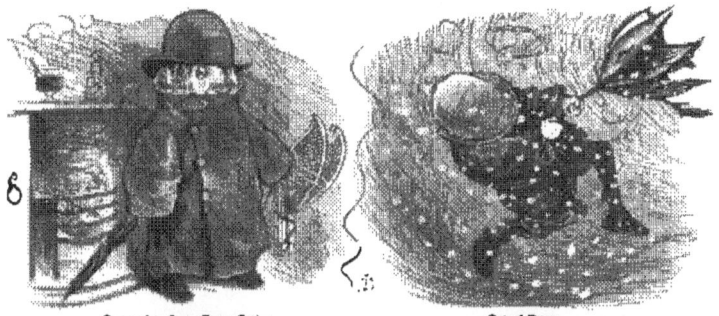

Preparations for an Easter Outing.

Out of Doors.

The Crush at the Railway Station.   Departure of the Excursion Train.

Exciting Scene at the Tea Gardens.

CHRISTMAS CHARITY.
A TALE OF A BLANKET.

ACT I. "How well it would look to make some poor shivering creature warm and comfortable this Christmas!"

"Oh, dear, that blanket is much too good! I want it for charitable purposes."

"This will be just the article, ma'am; you will perceive that it is quite transparent when held up to the light. It is the very worst quality made."

ACT II. "Precious cold, ain't it, Sal? Why, here's a kind lady with a blanket!"

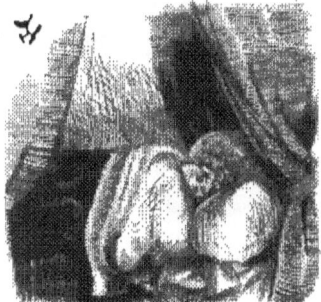

"Don't seem to make you much warmer, do it, though?"

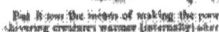

But it was the means of making the poor shivering creatures warmer (internally) after all!

ACT III. "How pleasant it is to reflect that those poor creatures are no longer shivering! Blankets are a great comfort!"

KING WINTER OUT OF HIS ELEMENT.

"What! Ice in the jug! Why, it must be freezing! Call me again when it isn't," said King Winter to the Clerk of the Weather; for he wasn't used to anything but slush, being an Englishman.

But it continued to freeze nevertheless, so he had to order a lot of overcoats, and get up.

He was miserably cold. "Who on earth is this unhappy old gentleman who won't skate or do anything but shiver?" every one asked.

It was no use to wrap himself up so I run about—he couldn't get warm! "Give me back my slush!" he said.

And a few days afterwards he was found frozen, all of a lump. The fact is, King Winter was simply a humbug exposed. Verdict, "Death from Exposure."

SOME NEW YEAR'S RESOLUTIONS.

"'Shure you I 've made sholemn d'termination not to tassh 'nother drop 'toxicatin' liquor. D'shanurm 'nish!"

"There—I will not eat so much next Christmas."

"I give in this time, my love, but next year I really must—ahem! with all respect—insist upon being master."

"This is very careless of me! I'm positively determined to take more care of myself in the future."

"Nothing on earth shall prevent my turning over a new leaf after this."

THE DEMON SKATER; OR, ALL LEGS AND WINGS.

A RECOLLECTION OF THE RINK.

THE BROAD GAUGE.

THE LEVEL CROSSING.

THE SEVEN-LEAGUED SKATER.

THE

BRITISH TRADESMAN

AND OTHER SKETCHES

INCLUDING

THE COMPLETE BUILDER

BY J. F. SULLIVAN

ENGRAVED BY DALZIEL BROTHERS

LONDON
"FUN" OFFICE, 153 FLEET STREET, E.C.
1880

ANNOUNCEMENT.

THIS Companion Volume to "THE BRITISH
WORKING MAN" is a second collection of Sketches
from the Pencil of J. F. SULLIVAN, culled from
the pages of "Fun."

"FUN" OFFICE,
FLEET STREET.

INTRODUCTION.

Lest any believe he's detected—
(The far-seeing elf!)
Some sketch in this volume directed
And aimed at himself;
This volume was never intended,
We vow, to make game
Of any whose cash is expended
In buying the same.

And this for an obvious reason
Not hard to surmise:—
'T were aimless and purposeless treason
To joke at THE WISE!
So, people who purchase these sketches,
And like them, and laugh,
We swear with an arm that upstretches,
We NEVER will chaff!

And as for the "Tradesman" selection.
Oh! let it not pass
As a foolish and sweeping reflection
That's aimed at a class
(A species of wit that engenders
A merited sneer!)—
But are there not truly offenders
In every sphere?

The Sketcher (who grieves, he confesses,
At making it known;
But loves to be candid) possesses
Some faults of his own:
And how can he view with displeasure
Trade's sorriest trait,
In view of the very short measure
These verses display?

JAMES F. SULLIVAN.

CONTENTS.

	PAGE
THE BRITISH TRADESMAN.	1
FLUCTUATIONS IN VALUE	15
THE VAGUE SCHOOL	16
ON NECKTIES	17
THE DEPRESSION IN TRADE	18
"MAKING A SHARP LAD OF HIM"	19
THE TAILOR	20
OUR MODERN BUGBEAR	21
THE ART OF CONVINCING	22
ABOUT AN UGLY VALENTINE	23
OUR MERCANTILE MARINE	24
PROTECTION TO FOREIGNERS; OR, THE HAND OF JUSTICE	25
THE SATIRIST'S VICTIM	26
AT A SERVANTS' REGISTRY OFFICE	27
PETS OR PESTS?	28
THE FOREBODING	29
THE FLOWER EXTERMINATOR	30
"IMPROVING" LANDSCAPES	31
THAT CAPITAL NOTION	32
A GREAT ADVANTAGE TO THE PUBLIC	33
ARMORIAL BEARINGS	34
RACE NOTES	35
THE ROAD TO REFORMATION	36
THE "RIGHTS" OF OUR RAILWAY COMPANIES	37
AT THE FOREIGN OFFICE	38
"A COMPLETE REST FOR THE BRAIN"	39
"GREAT EXCITEMENT PREVAILS"	40
LUGGAGE WORSHIP	41
THE HOLIDAY SEASON	42
SELFISHNESS?	43
THE PIPE-DEVOTEE	44
THE AMATEUR'S PLANT	45
ALL THAT CONFOUNDED CLIMATE!	46
OUR STATUES AGAIN	47
THE BUCOLIC BUGBEAR	48
"QUITE AN ART IN ITSELF!"	49
OUR PROTECTORS!	50
THE VICTIMS OF LIMELIGHT	51
RATHER AN IMPORTANT PERSONAGE	52
OUR ANNUAL SACRIFICE	53
THE TRADESMEN OF OUR SUBURB	54
USEFUL GRANDMOTHERLY GOVERNMENT	55
ON THE TRAIL	64
OH, THAT MANCHESTER!	69
THE PENALTY OF FAME	70
REVENGE IS SWEET	71
THE BETRAYER	72
THE IMPOSTOR	73
THE "POLITICAL" INCUBUS	74
THE DIFFICULTIES OF SOME GENERALS	75
FROM SOUTH AFRICA AGAIN	76
THE POLITICAL OFFENDER IN RUSSIA	77
AN UNPRECEDENTED LARK	78
TERMS FOR THE TOW-PATH	79
OUR GAS	80
OUR BENEFIT SOCIETY	81
A QUESTION OF TITLE	82
FURTHER SUNDAY READING	83
TURFISM TURNED TOPSY-TURVY	84
OUR NATIONAL FAULT	85
THE CRUSHING BUS-DRIVER	86
BEAUTIFUL EXAMPLE OF COMPUNCTION	87
THE MYSTERIOUS ATTRACTION	88
ECCENTRICITIES OF THE ELECTRIC CURRENT	89
THE BOOK BORROWER	90
BOOKS AGAIN	91
"TO SUIT ALL CUSTOMERS"	92
THE RIGHT PRINCIPLE	93
GARDENING FOR 1899	94
THE COMPLETE BUILDER	95

THE
BRITISH TRADESMAN;
AND
OTHER SKETCHES.

No. 1.—THE BUTCHER'S LATEST LITTLE JOKE.

The dangers of carrying a brown-paper parcel through the streets.

NO. 2—THE INNKEEPER'S LITTLE JOKE.

"Tired and hungry, sir—anything to eat, sir?" "Any blessed thing you please to order, sir—any blessed thing!"

"Chicken, sir?" "Well—s—no, o. That 's a thing we don't 'appen to 'ave. Anything else in creation."

"Eggs—cold meat—soup—chop—steak!" "Well, no—we 're out o' them too, you see."

"What have we? Well, sir—we can offer you a nice cut o' bread an' cheese."

"Not satisfied with bread an' cheese! Actooally goin' away! Well, he thinks nothin' of himself, he does!"

No. 9.—THE OUTFITTER'S LITTLE JOKE.

" '*In a great hurry,' sir?*—Yes, sir. '*Pair of gloves,' sir?*—'*Be quick,' sir?*—Certainly, sir."

"Let me see—'er, 'gloves,' you said? I couldn't recommend any neat little thing in this way, I suppose?'"

"Oh—ah, yes—gloves, of course. Now, here's a sweet thing in dressing-gowns!"

" ' *Can't wait,' sir?*—Well, the fact is we 're out of gloves just now, you see, but—'"

No. 4.—THE BOOTMAKER'S LITTLE JOKE.

"A pair of boots for the young lady, sir? *Certainly, sir.* You shall have them, without fail, on *Tuesday.*"

(*An interval of twelve years. Enter the Young Lady, arrived at Womanhood.*)

"Them boots your papa ordered, miss? Well, miss—no, not quite done—but you shall have them to-morrow, for certain."

(*Another interval, of fifteen years. Enter the Young Lady with her Daughter.*)

"Well, mum—no; but I expect 'em in every minute. Eh, mum?—Well, no, I'd confess they ain't begun yet—but you shall." &c., &c.

(*A further interval, of ninety years.*) "I've brought them boots as were ordered of my grandfather, for a young lady. What! whole family extinct? Well, but—I want my money!"

4

No. 5.—THE POULTERER'S LITTLE JOKE.

"Now, sir, here's a splendid turkey! Let me send you this one. Thank you, sir. I'll send it round immediately."

"If you want a turkey, ma'am, this is the thing for you. Your address, ma'am? Thank you; you shall have it in a quarter of an hour."

"Want a turkey, d' you? Can't do better than have this one. Weighs nearly a ton! Send it round to you? All right, thankee."

"What! Mean to tell me I ain't sent the turkeys you ordered? Oh, you're a-making a mistake. Do you mean to tell me I ain't honest? What next!!"

No. 6.—THE BUTCHER'S LITTLE JOKE.

"Not sent in your bill for two years, sir? Well, you see, we don't like to bother our customers with bills; but of course you can have it if you wish."

"Not sent your bill in yet, sir? Oh, dear me, no—I quite forgot it; but of course if you really want——"

"' You'll turn bankrupt if I don't send in your bill?' Oh, dear, I shouldn't like to give you that trouble. Our customers don't generally like, &c., but of course if you prefer," &c.

"Sent your bill at last, sir? Yes, sir. What I jot down things you 'aven't 'ad? Didn't 'ave two oxen on Christmas Day, 1864?—also ten sheep on Good Friday, 1865?—nor six calves on the following Monday?—nor three tons o' sirloin on the next Wensday?—nor twenty lambs——? Oh, you must 'a 'ad 'em. There they are, down in the bill, yer know!"

No. 7,—THE WINE-MERCHANT'S LITTLE JOKE.

"I know what you want! Here's the very thing—a rich, full-bodied wine—something with a backbone in it, eh? I'll send you a few dozen from this cask."

"I see—I see. What you require is a sound, elegant, dry wine: as light as possible. Something that leaves the palate at once—that's it. Here it is exactly. We'll bottle just off a stanch or two from this cask."

"I say, old boy, come and dine with me. I've the richest, most elegant, driest, lightest wine you ever saw in your life. Leaves the palate at once, sir—think of that!"

"Um! yes, your dry wine isn't so bad, but—it can't compare with something I've just got in. Rich, sir! ah! and full-bodied. Backbone in it, sir!"

No. 8.—THE LITTLE SEASONABLE GIFT JOKE.

"Can't get rid of that article. You see, people won't look at it."

"Now *that* plan ought to do, oughtn't it? But no, people won't look at it yet."

No. 8.—WHAT BUTCHERS WILL BE.

BY OUR ANGRY HOUSEHOLDER.

"Why, sir, things are coming to such a pass that butchers will set up in business in this way next!"

"And the customers will have to wait on him for patronage, and leave their cards with his page!"

"We shall have the credit system reversed, they pay ready money for our meat and wait till we get it!"

"And how about a bad debt then!"

No. 10.—THE "TIRING 'EM OUT" SYSTEM.

"I want you to make me a tall, black, narrow-brimmed chimney pot hat, precisely like this one I have on."

"Made it, have you? Well—a—but—that's not exactly like mine; that's a short, white, broad-brimmed country-man's hat!"

"Tried again, eh? Well, but—look here; you can see the difference with the naked eye! This is a short, grey billycock."

"Hang it! This is farther off still—it's a cork helmet."

"'Can't make it any newer than this?' Why, conf——. Oh, there—this'll do!!!"

No. 11.—A CRY FROM THE OPPRESSED.

Our Tradesman very justly complains that no manner has he got his wares nicely laid out

Than some stupid Cabman is certain to get involved in a bedstead (and fittings, complete, £6 2s. 11d., a bargain !) ; or some idiotic pedestrian is sure to tumble over a chest of drawers (unequalled, solid mahogany, 19s. 3d.!) ; and as to paying for 'em, not they.

Why, he says somebody actually had the coolness to get going in a rage the other day, on the pretence that our Tradesman's goods (warranted London-made) created an obstruction ! Just as if he couldn't have going round by the next turning ; and the worst of it is, the very police encourage the public in this system of persecution ! The largest stock of chairs, settees, &c. in London.— [ADVT.]

No. 12.—A HINT ON THE ACQUISITION OF PAVEMENT.

When an exposer of wares has set his mind on acquiring any piece of public pavement, he should take a hint from the example of Lords of the Manor, and commence his enclosure with a low fence of unobtrusively small articles.

After a time the fence may be somewhat increased in height; and again, after a further period,

No. 18.—LAYING OUT WARES AGAIN.

Capital notion for a Seaside Draper.   Only a question of difficulty.

Terrible misfortune that happened to our friend Jones.   He got built up among some wares, and has never been seen since.

No. 14.—FITTING ONE WITH A HAT.

The Gentleman with a rather large head.

The hat that will be a capital fit if you just allow me to ease it on a little, sir.

The result.

The Gentleman with a rather small head.

The hat that will fit like a skin when I've just put in a little pad, sir.

The result.

In conclusion, a word of solid advice to all about to be fitted with a hat. Do not have a head either unusually large or uncommonly small, but of a moderate and medium size. If possible, find out the usual average size of your Hatter's hats, and model your head accordingly.

FLUCTUATIONS IN VALUE.
BY OUR SPECIAL PURCHASER.

To the Trade :—" Vell, I'm afraid we can't do thorthe for you for leth than ten unnderngth a-peeth ; you thee, it'th the materiel that'th the vallyble."

Rising in value.

To the Public :—Knut. "We can let you have this for fifteen guineas, sir. You perceive that it is the workmanship—and the style— whish cost us so much."

THE VAGUE SCHOOL.

"Well," said his friend, "I won't deceive you, Pallet. I'm afraid it's not much like a landscape, but it would make a splendid battle scene with a touch here and there."

So Pallet put a few rapid touches to make a battle scene of it. "There now!" he said.

"O-o-oh! You've quite altered it now!" said his friend. "But it would make a perfect shipwreck with a couple of touches here."

So Pallet made a shipwreck of it; and they accepted it at the Academy; and a connoisseur, who was a magnificent judge, came along, and exclaiming, "That's a masterly bit of portrait-painting!" bought it at once.

ON NECKTIES.

"Cravat come to pieces, sir? Impossible! I assure you they are all tested, and will bear a strain of three tons. Try *this one, sir.*"

"*This* cravat come to pieces, sir? Impossible! There must be some mistake! Will you try with *this one?* I 'm sure you 'll find this one will last for ever!" (*And so on through generations.*)

THE DEPRESSION IN TRADE.

" I assure you, Miss, business is so bad that I have been compelled to enlarge my establishment and put larger plate-glass throughout."

" You'll believe me, Ma'am, at this price there is no profit whatever. I have so much by it that I have been driven to the extremity of engaging two hundred extra assistants."

" My dear young lady, it was useless to struggle against fate. Business got so bad that I was positively forced to purchase this villa and retire !"

"MAKING A SHARP LAD OF HIM."
(AS IT IS DONE IN THE CITY.)

The raw material.

The patent chest-contracting and back-deforming process.

The warranted after-breakfast-rushing-to-town-digestion-ruining process.

THE TAILOR.

"You see that gentleman just going out? *My best customer, sir!* Wouldn't lose him for the world!—

Just fitted out all his relations and friends with new overcoats." (*A mad elapse.*)

"I told you about that customer of mine, sir? Well," (joyfully,) "he's *dead!* Got to fit out all his relations and friends with superfine mourning. All three new overcoats 'ill have to be thrown away." (*Rubs his hands and chuckles.*)

OUR MODERN BUGBEAR.

Portrait of a "Brick of a Fellow" who will go for a walk in any weather.

Temptation.

Weakness.

Portrait of a Miserable Plat?ronan who shrinks from weather of any kind.

Patent glass shade for keeping dust, soot, rain, and hail from the Bugbear; fitted with protector frame to defend the glass shade from damage, and fancy fly-papers to attract insects from the Bugbear.

A few portable accessories for keeping the Bugbear in good condition—box, hat-brush, gross, furnace to heat same, silk handkerchief, large umbrella, &c., &c. Absolutely essential to those who wear screw-pipe hats.

THE ART OF CONVINCING.

"You would wish for one in plain white, Miss? Oh, certainly.
Plain white—quite so !"

"This, I think, will be exactly what you are pleased to require ?
I think you will find this article plain white."

" 'Dots on it,' Miss? Oh, dear me, no ! I do not perceive any
dots on it."

"If you will look at it without prejudice, in this light, you will perceive
there is no pattern on it.—Besides, it will wash out at once."

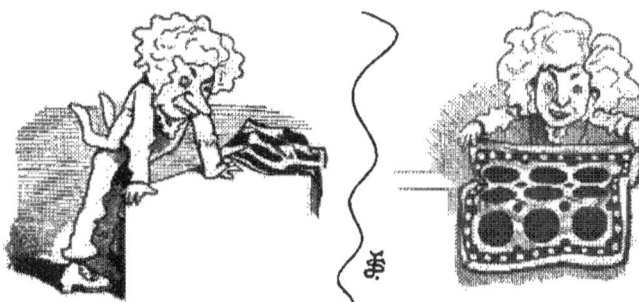

"I do not think I could recommend anything plainer, Miss; and, in
fact, this is the only article we have in stock."

" 'You must have it either quite plain or very loud !' This is just the
thing, then—I couldn't show you anything louder than this."

ABOUT AN UGLY VALENTINE.

OUR MERCANTILE MARINE.

A sketch on Tower Hill. Embryo Murderers waiting for a job.

The best means of "preserving life" (i.e., the Captain's life) "at sea."

The Ironclad Skipper—a hint to Officers in the Merchant Service.

PROTECTION TO FOREIGNERS; or, The Hand of Justice.

In the happy land of England, a German Workman goes forth to his work, comfortably assured that there at least is safety for the stranger.

Somehow, however, it appears to be otherwise.

And the presumptuous foreigner has to learn that he will not be permitted to draw a weapon—or in fact do anything—in self-defence, without incurring the most terrible penalties !

THE SATIRIST'S VICTIM.

AN ENTIRELY EGOTISTICAL NARRATIVE.

There was an Artist who completed a most satirical—nay, iron nay, sarcastic—caricature of an enemy.

And he watched the Victim as he purchased the periodical in which was the caricature; and

He tracked him to a restaurant to enjoy his agony.

But the Victim gazed at the caricature, and a smile spread over his features,

And the smile broadened out until it became a great laugh.

"Have you seen this sketch, sir?" said the Victim. "The funniest thing I've seen for a long time—all about me!"

So the Comic Artist completed a caricature of himself, and was heard of no more.

"I am not fair," he, moaning, said,
"My eyebrows lack the classic arch,
There lurks no grace about my head."
(He spoke a year ago—in March.)
"I 'm sure to get," he said, "I fear,
An ugly Valentine next year."

With dread Foreboding's dismal wing,
O'erspread above him like a pall,
He bought supplies of patent things
To beautify himself withal.

"Perchance," he mused, whene'er head
In-terven a change such as mine;
By this I might avoid the dread
Anticipated Valentine,"

But no! with all his patent balsam,
With shaven head, with flowing hair,
This dread foreboding knew no calms;
The year advanced—he wooed despair.

Then February came at last,
The looming future seemed to mock,
Foreboding culminated fast,
And then—and then—the Postman's knock!

"I aimed myself—Despair! he moan!"
He said. "My nerves shall shame a rock." • • •
It was a pretty Valentine,
His own—it was RICH OLDSON'S shock.

THE FLOWER EXTERMINATOR.

This gives you the Patriot known to the Parks,
Displaying his views in enlightened remarks;
He kindly instructs, in his able address,
The Cabinet, Russia, the Ports, and the Press.

Now, let us suppose that the Cabinet met,
And decided to follow the rules that he set;
Repented directly, with terror determined,
To rigidly follow his thrilling sermon!

We'll further imagine the Ports to decide
To look upon him as their leader and guide;

We'll also imagine the Ports and the Czar
Agreeing to make him their governing star.

And then we'll imagine that Patriot's state—
We'll fancy him sitting and cursing his fate,   Without an excuse for impressing his mark
On crocuses, tulips, and trees in the Park!   And fancy the flowers uninjured and bright—
And fancy our unpatriotic delight!

AT A SERVANTS' REGISTRY OFFICE.

Lady in search of Servants. "I require a cook, a housemaid, and a scullery-maid
—but this scullery-maid will not suit me."
                                                    [*Exit Girl.*

(Returns Girl.) Girl. "I think you wanted a
'ousemaid, mum?"
Lady. "Yes, but surely you 're the same girl that
came to me as a scullery-maid just now?"
Girl. "Yes, mum; but yer see, I 've washed my
face and put on some tidy bow, and these yere
gloves,—and then I 'm a 'ousemaid."

"And when I bllge my 'air a bit extry
—then I 'm a cook."

The Registry Office Keeper. "Well, mm'um, she is all the stock we have at present,
and she 's sure to be snapped up, unless you decide at once."
                                                    [*Lady does decide at once—*" No !"

1. Is an amiable lady, who, putting down her newspaper in horror, delates upon the scandalousness of allowing so many dogs to run about the streets and annoy everybody.

2. Represents three of the amiable lady's pet cats doing a chorus outside a next door window (invalid within).

3. Is a sketch of the route taken next door but one by another of her pets, with notes by the way:—(A) Dusthole, newly painted black. (B) Steps (just whitened). (C) Conservatory, newly painted white. (D) Side of house, newly painted stone-colour.

4. Shows another of her pets with booty from next door but two.

5. Gives another of her pets maturing a scheme next door but three.

While 6 sets forth yet another pet throwing up earthworks on a neat flower-bed at next door but four.

"IMPROVING" LANDSCAPES.

[Before the Select Committee on the Thirlmere Water Scheme, Mr. Frank Buckland expressed an opinion that " It would rather improve the Lake, as people would go to see the wonderful engineering works which had been erected." (!!!) We humbly suggest a few more plans for "improving" scenery.]

A few nice chimney-stacks at our seaside resorts, to be kept smoking "Daily during the Season."

Capital centre ornament for a flower-garden—Gas-works in full swing.

Nice soap factories here and there on the Swiss mountains.

Drainage pipes (purely for ornamental purposes) in Windsor and other Forests.

THAT CAPITAL NOTION
OF BRANDING EVERY ONE IN THE ARMY, IN ORDER TO PREVENT DESERTION!!!

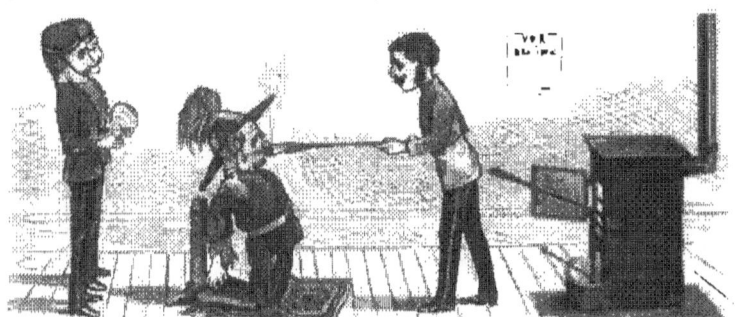

Pleasing little incident in the career of a Field Officer !

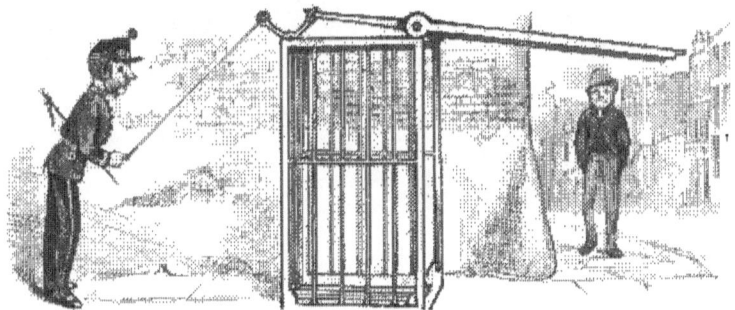

Novel plan of recruiting, rendered necessary by

A GREAT ADVANTAGE TO THE PUBLIC.

"Hooray!" said the Public, reading its paper, "such lots of American beef coming over! We shall get our meat at a fair price now, and the butchers will be brought to their senses."

But somehow there was a not unhappy twinkle in the Butcher's eye when he read of the American beef, and he was observed to buy no more live stock.

"I'll just call round on the Butcher and jeer at him in his adversity," said the Public. And it did this thing; but the Butcher still preserved a gay unnatural calm.

And many days the Public looked about for cheapened meat, and for the advantage to accrue from the American beef, but found not what it sought. In despair it went to the Butcher. "Do you know where all the American beef goes to?" it cried. "No, I'm sure I don't know anything about it," said the innocent Butcher; "I don't believe any's arrived!" But his eye was gay.

ARMORIAL BEARINGS.

When you owe anybody a grudge, bribe a likely little boy

To chalk a picture on his (the anybody's) back ;   Then make an appointment to meet him outside the Inland Revenue Office.

You will have your revenge ! The Lynx-eyed Authorities will instantly swoop upon him for wearing armorial bearings without a license, and we dare not think what 'll be done to him.

THE ROAD TO REFORMATION.

[WITH APOLOGIES TO MR. FRITH, R.A.]

Interruption.

Discharged with a caution—a pitiable case; something from
the poor-box.

Improving circumstances—the street lecturer.

Remorse—enormous receipts.

Up again.

THE "RIGHTS" OF OUR RAILWAY COMPANIES.

Imaginative homage to the rights of the London and North-Western Railway Company.—Crossing their line in the air to which they have the sole claim! Prompt and energetic action of the local station-master.

The Latest from the same Company:—"Very sorry, gents, but I've strict orders to poke this little chimney under the nose of everybody as looks over the line, to prevent them thinking they 've a right to do it twenty years hence."

AT THE FOREIGN OFFICE.
A GREAT SECRET.

"Hush!" said an official at the F. O., "I have a diplomatic document of great importance. Its contents are a profound secret. Can we be overheard?"

"Let us speak in a whisper. There it is. We had better close the shutters."

Then all the confidential clerks were called in and bound by a great oath to secrecy.

"Hallo!" said the official next in bigness, "all the confidential clerks are busy; there is no one to copy this document. Messenger, run out and call in the first person you see to copy this secret and important memorandum."

And they found somebody at once, and paid him sixpence. * * *
And after all THIS precaution the secret actually leaked out!!!

38

"A COMPLETE REST FOR THE BRAIN."

"My love," said the overworked Poet, "the brain grows weary;

So we will put away all brain labour, and give the brain a month's complete rest."

"So, here is the Railway Time-book; let us see where we can go, and when."

Ah! here is a train which leaves London at 9 a.m., and arrives at Plymouth two hours before; and here is another which catches another which starts from before it arriving and here is another which leaves London at 2 p.m., and arrives at the middle of its journey at 12.30 p.m., calling at this and at the journey on the way; and here 's——

So he just settled himself to puzzle the matter out, and——

"Halla!" he said, suddenly; "why, the month 's up, and I must return to my work; but I 've given my brain a nice rest."

"GREAT EXCITEMENT PREVAILS."

First Loafer (to Second). "There's a feller a-dyin' ov starvation jest round the corner—can't git inter the work'us ; rum go, ain't it?"

First Gentleman (to Second). "Oh, by the way, saw a very curious sight coming along—fellow actually dying of starvation on the pavement ; very interesting thing to see."

First Charitable Lady (to Second). "Would you believe it? There was a dreadful man so shockingly vulgar as to be dying of starvation as I drove here!"

First Boy (to Second). "Oh, I say, such a lark ; bin a-lookin' at a cove a-dyin' of starvation!"

Extract from subsequent newspaper report.—"The unfortunate man was at length conveyed to the workhouse, where he expired immediately. Great excitement and indignation prevail in the neighbourhood."

LUGGAGE WORSHIP.

"Boots," scolded the newly-arrived hotel visitor, "why did the Landlord send
me up, under the care of the sub-deputy-under-supernumerary-scullery-maid, to
the worst attic in the hotel? I am a Duke, and very rich; I want a suite of
rooms." "It's 'cos you've on'y got one little portmanteau," said the Boots.

So the Duke cunningly sneaked out, returned by the next
omnibus, and stood by a pile of other people's luggage.

The Landlord advanced obsequiously.

The Landlord himself conducted the visitor to his grandest suite of rooms.

THE HOLIDAY SEASON.

GRAND EXTRA SPECIAL RAILWAY ARRANGEMENTS FOR TOURISTS!!

SELFISHNESS?

"Of course, we couldn't go out of town without taking baby! And we never found him the least worry."

"We always put down out baby in another compartment, and his stomach face it.... keep him windowers, and tied out, let him one handles... and gave her glorify of wraps, and a portable kitchen food cooker, and asked him going to in the carriage and to talk, so he doesn't like being looked at."

"And baby always travelled at the back of the coach, so he didn't worry us at all."

"And we always sent him on to the other deck on the river steamers; so his crying (as I he cries a great deal, poor darling') never worried us; so jo not rationa-and-anual that some disagreeable people can object to babies travelling!"

THE PIPE-DEVOTEE.

He had a lovely new pipe; the question was " Where to take it for its holiday?"

He tried the seaside at first; but the wind began to colour the poor thing all on one side.

So he rushed inland; but the sun in the midlands began to scorch the dear, and this was not *legitimate colouring.*

So he tried Scotland; but the mists disagreed with the bobby.

THE AMATEUR'S PLANT.

There must be a kind of fatality hanging over the plants of an amateur planticulturist. He buys a magnificent specimen. Very well. The thing requires a warm equable temperature to begin with.

Very well. He arranges such conditions for it, keeping the gas always on, that the temperature may not vary. Yet it droops!

It wants re-potting. Very well. He re-pots it every day—(none of your nasty common flower-pots with a hole in the bottom, but expensive non-porous china and gold vases!) Yet it droops!

He builds a greenhouse for it, and only leaves the windows open in one or two hard frosts. Yet it goes and dies!

ALL THAT CONFOUNDED CLIMATE!

We resolved to preserve a statue in *our* climate. Only a year ago we put up a beautiful statue; and we stationed two policemen to keep off boys;

And I we hired a man to scrape it hard every week with chisels;

And yet that statue's surface seemed to gradually wear away. Oh, that climate!

So we hired a stronger man to scrape the statue every day with bigger chisels;

But, would you believe it? the surface seemed to actually wear away *faster than ever*! All that climate. We've ordered a patent steam scraper, warranted to scrape away a ton an hour, and if *that* won't preserve the statue—we'll—!

OUR STATUES AGAIN.
A SUGGESTION.

The gradual reduction of the bulk of statues by the process of scraping—we mean by our climate—might be turned to account, thus:—

Let every statue, when first made, represent a person of great bulk—
for example, the "Claimant";

After a period of reduction, it might be converted into a likeness of
Her Majesty;

After more reduction, it might take the form of—say Earl
Beaconsfield;

Again, after more scraping—ahem! *stimulating*—going, it might set forth
the elegantly slim figure of—say Mr. Fun;

Anon it might reduce itself to a amusement of the living
skeleton;

And it would finally do excellently for a lamp-post. At this stage it could
be left dirty—and preserved.

THE BUCOLIC BUGBEAR

(A RECORD OF A SKETCHER'S SENSATIONS.)

As soon as you've chosen a nice bit, the Bugbear sneaks up to peep.

You can hear looking over riverbank, dead trunk or a fence; then he seems to scrutinise all against you. At first he carefully crawls when passing in front, in order not to interrupt your view;

He glances through the fence; he maddens you.

Then he grows bolder. He poses to be "drawn," and blots out the whole landscape; in despair you at length "draw" him as ugly as possible—THEN

If he doesn't send all his friends to be "drawed!"

"QUITE AN ART IN ITSELF!"

"You will notice," says the Photographic Artist, "the immense variety of the poses in my photographs. Quite an art in itself to pose the subjects! I shall be able to make a first-rate picture of you!"

"You see, I place you first in my patent posing machine—that machine's quite an art in itself, too——."

"Then, by simply turning a handle or two, I screw you at once into a most natural and picturesque pose—quite an art. Put a little more expression into the features, please."

"What? 'Don't think the machine quite suits you?' 'Not a natural pose?' 'Would rather sit easily in a chair, so?' Oh, my dear sir, most preposterous! Wouldn't do at all! No ART in it. Oh, dear, you'll excuse my laughing at the notion!"

OUR—PROTECTORS!

Feeling the way.—Belated citizens in Piccadilly, November, 1878.

The imprudent party who called for the police ;   And regretted it.

A little suggestion. Suppose the inhabitants of Piccadilly swore in a few *professional gentlemen* as special constables to keep their "protectors" in order ?

THE VICTIMS OF LIMELIGHT.

On the next Christmas Eve but one, the usual belated traveller urged his jaded steed across the customary Haunted Heath. His terrified gaze searched in vain for the regular Christmas Spectre. The fact was the whole earth was lighted up every night with limelight;

And the Regular Spectre struggled in vain to appear; for there was no inch of darkness anywhere for it to appear in.

"I can't help you," said the Christmas Ghost-Story Writer. "I'm ruined by this limelight. I can't write any more stories—I can't get on without my darkness!"

And, sure enough, he had to put up all his "effects" to auction; and they fetched very little.

RATHER AN IMPORTANT PERSONAGE!

(SOME *IMPRESSIONS*, ON READING ARTICLES ABOUT "OUR CORRESPONDENT" IN THE PAPERS.)

1. "Our Correspondent and the officers around him."
2. "Our Correspondent expressed his decided opinion to the Commander-in-Chief."
3. "Our Correspondent and the Generals A., B., and C. having followed up the convoy."
4. "The foe immediately evacuated the fort on the approach of our Correspondent, as I——" (let the other personages are of no consequence).
5. "On the arrival of our Correspondent the War commenced."

OUR ANNUAL SACRIFICE.

" You ought to invite Jones to turkey and pudding, this Christmas," whispered the Fiend Dyspepsia to Brown, " for friendship's sake. He's so fond of turkey and pudding!" Now Brown loathed turkey and pudding—still, out of respect for Jones's whim, why—

"You must accept Brown's invite to the turkey and pudding," whispered the kverpouy Fiend to Jones; "only friendly, you know, considering how he adores turkey and pudding!" Now, if Jones abhorred two things in this world, those things were turkey and pudding;—yet, as Brown loved 'em so, why—

And these two friendly men sacrificed their feelings and ate heavy things out of pure consideration for each other's inclinations. And that night the obscured designing Fiend gave 'em a good time of it! The two never cared for each other after that—they avoided each other; don't even bow now.

RATHER AN IMPORTANT PERSONAGE!

(SOME *IMPRESSIONS*, ON READING ARTICLES ABOUT "OUR CORRESPONDENT" IN THE PAPERS.)

1. "Our Correspondent and the officers around him."
2. "Our Correspondent expressed his decided opinion to the Commander-in-Chief."
3. "Our Correspondent and the Generals A., B., and C. having followed up the enemy."
4. "The foe immediately evacuated the fort on the approach of our Correspondent, as I——' (but the other personages are of no consequence)."
5. "On the arrival of our Correspondent the War commenced."

OUR ANNUAL SACRIFICE.

"You *ought* to invite Jones to turkey and pudding, this Christmas," whispered the Fiend Dyspepsia to Brown. "For friendship's sake. He's so fond of turkey and pudding ! Now Brown loathed turkey and pudding—still, out of respect for Jones's whim, why—

"You *must* accept Brown's invite to the turkey and pudding," whispered the foregoing Fiend to Jones ; "only friendly, you know, considering how he adores turkey and pudding ! " Now Jones abhorred two things in this world, those things were turkey and pudding ;—yet, as Brown loved 'em so, why—

And these two friendly men sacrificed their feelings and ate heavy things out of pure consideration for each other's inclinations. And that night the obscured designing Fiend gave 'em a good time of it ! The two never cared for each other after that—they avoided each other ; don't even bow now.

THE TRADESMEN OF OUR SUBURB.
THEIR PECULIARITIES.

"Umbrella, sir? No, we haven't any in stock; and, in fact, you won't get one anywhere; no such things made; don't exist; don't believe there ever were such things!"

(Then you purchase one elsewhere, and show it to him—thus :)— "Bought one, sir? Oh, dear no; you must be mistaken; that's not an umbrella—they can't be got anywhere."

"'Soiled,' Miss? Well, the fact is our customers will not buy cuffs and collars unless they're a little soiled—always ask for soiled ones, I assure you!"

"'Last month's last one's magazines,' sir? Oh, they're out one yes, but we shall have them in a fortnight or so."

"The fact is, mum, you see, our cart from Covent Garden has to pay sixpence to get over the bridge, so that we're obliged to put sixpence extra on each plant to cover it."

USEFUL GRANDMOTHERLY GOVERNMENT.

OUR HOPELESSLY-IDIOTIC-JURYMEN SUPPRESSION BILL.

When any Juryman shall be found to have recommended to mercy more than six deliberate and brutal murderers, that Juryman shall receive a sanitary visit from a qualified medical inspector,

Who shall proceed to examine his phrenological development, and pronounce upon the severity of the case.

Should he consider it a case of aggravated Idiocy, that unfortunate Juryman shall be placed under complete official supervision,

And should he be found to persist in his pernicious course, he shall be handed over to the Local murderers, and recommended to his mercy.

GRANDMOTHERLY GOVERNMENT ASLEEP.

The Government had for some time past been peacefully dreaming about muzzling little dogs and preventing folks getting tipsy,

When she was suddenly awakened by a great bang!

"Deary—deary—deary!" she said; "there's a dreadful smash! But who'd have thought of five tons of gunpowder going off like that?"

Still her conscience wasn't easy, so she consulted that M.P. of ours.

"What I regulate the carriage of explosives!" he exclaimed; "I fear any law on the subject would be so absurdly simple and definite that the people would understand it."

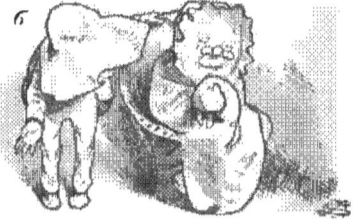

"Ah! that wouldn't do," she mused. "You just go to sleep again till you're woke by another great bang—and then we'll talk about it," he said. And we suppose she will.

GRANDMOTHERLY GOVERNMENT.

OUR GRANDMOTHERLY M.P.'S NIGHTMARE.

Our Grandmotherly M.P. had been reading so intently the opinions of the Press in respect of recent doings in the House,

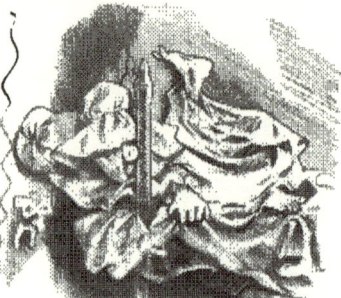

That when he returned to bed, he was quite frightened and restless ;

Convinced that an Irish Member was under the bed, muttering something about "disreputable band," and threatening to fight him

And he could not get away from that Irish Member,

Who would beg him to choose a revolver and state his distance.

And when our M.P. woke up, he was just withdrawing all the expressions he had used, and shaking hands over it.

We hasten to explain to all Irish Members that this is intended entirely in a Pickwickian sense. *But we're a dead shot.*

OUR GRANDMOTHERLY M.P. AND THE SILLY SEASON.

He was so absorbed in the latest bit of padding about Poutoppidan and the Monster Kraken that he really hadn't noticed where he sat down.

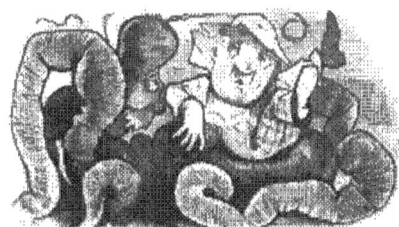

" Awful book all this about polype, ain't it ? " said a voice, so close to his elbow that he almost started.

" Now you 'd hardly credit that *I* was a newspaper writer once ! But I was. *I* used to twaddle about the Kraken in the silly season till I dreamed about it ! "

" And I used to brood about it till I brooded myself into one. And if others I know on don't look out, they may get took the same way ; so just you look——"

But our M. P.'s chance had come, and he bolted like mad   * * * * *

" Hello ! " he said ; " nearly two hours ! but I suppose it 's the fresh air." Still, he hasn't forgotten his mention to the newspaper writers.

A FEW MORE GRANDMOTHERLY BILLS.

Overjoyed by the interesting sobriety resulting from liquor legislation, we offer hints for the forcible encouragement of other Christian Virtues :—

HUMILITY.—Every well-to-do citizen shall clean his own boots once a week.

PATIENCE.—Anybody caught hurrying anywhere shall be tied to the nearest lamp-post for ten minutes.

ABSTEMIOUSNESS.— All eating-houses and sweetstuff shops shall close at 5 p.m. ; and

Babies convicted of consuming more than 1 lb. of lollipops at once shall be run in.

MODERATION.—Nobody shall smoke more than three pipes in one day.

INDUSTRY.—All citizens shall be up at 6 a.m.

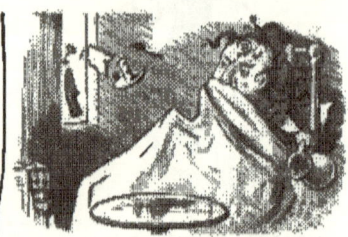

AMIABILITY.—Any one resenting the latter law shall be liable to imprisonment.

STILL A FEW MORE.

Having successfully encouraged the Christmas Virtues mentioned before, we might then proceed to enforce a little—

VEGETATION.—Any one meeting at our Public Monuments, to be run in.

PERSEVERANCE.—Folks failing to obtain immediate parochial relief, to keep on trying till they get it.

TRUTHFULNESS.—No change needed here—merely stick to the Income Tax.

HUMANITY.—No change here either. Leave the Railway Companies to their little games.

UNIVERSAL VIRTUE (and convenient supposed). Let the Comic Artists legislate for the country, or make Peers of 'em.

OUR GLUTTONY-ABOLITION (MIDDLE-AGED GENTLEMEN) BILL.

By OUR SPECIAL M.P.

When any public officer (dressed in plain clothes, and placed in some inconspicuous place of observation,)

Shall discover any individual whose personal obesity would indicate excessive indulgence in solid nutriment,

He shall trace that individual to his place of residence;

And (armed with a warrant) warn that individual's cook as to limiting that individual's future supply of alimentary substances.

The pastrycooks, within a radius of two miles, shall also be cautioned against pandering to his cravings for the edible.

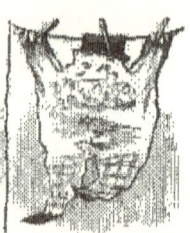

After a time, should that individual's bulk be found to augment,

He shall be summoned and fined whenever he is found at large.

And, should such correction fail, he shall be rolled out flat, and hung up conspicuously as an EXAMPLE.

THE ELIGIBLE-YOUNG-MEN-WITH-NO-INTENTIONS ANNIHILATION BILL.

In the case of any eligible young gentleman being suspected of having no matrimonial intentions,

One of a staff of properly-qualified Detectives

Shall interview him, and, if possible, so work upon his feelings

As to cause him to offer attentions to her;

Upon which she shall reveal the object of her errand, and denounce him before the nearest Magistrate;

When he shall, on being convicted of FLIRTATION WITHOUT ULTI-MATE MATRIMONIAL VIEWS, be married by force to one of a staff of spinsters specially retained by Government for that purpose.

OUR GRANDMOTHERLY M.P. IN THE RECESS.

He was enjoying, by the foaming billow, a little light literature in the shape of the laws of England,

When he suddenly came across an Act without any amendments or complications.

" Why, this is shameful ! " he said ; " my very landlady could understand this ! " And it was a scandalous fact, sic ! His very landlady could !

" This must be altered ! " he said, and set about repealing and amending it, with an eye to next Session.

" There," he said, " is 'll puzzle the old lady now."

" That's what we M.P.'s call a law of England, ma'am ! Now it 'll match the other laws, ma'am. Stay—there 's just one more amendment which I——" and he set to work again.

OUR GRANDMOTHERLY M.P. AND THE NIGGERS.

Our M.P., although the Irish Member no longer haunts him, has, nevertheless, been anxious and sleepless lately.

He has been rescuing a lot of little niggers on the East Coast of Africa, and now he doesn't know how to get rid of them.

He has offered them to the Commissioners of Paving to pave the roads of the metropolis with, and thus put an end to the asphalte-kyro-cobble-stone difficulty. But the Commissioners can not make up their minds.

So our M.P. thinks he will have to make City clerks of the males and governesses of the females. It will be a change of slavery—and change is always agreeable.

OUR M.P. IN A FRIGHT.

"Good gracious! What is that noise at the door?" gasped our M.P.   "Why, here's a lady attempting to get into THE HOUSE! Oh dear!"

"My dear madam, you CAN'T come in here!!! Consider my character, pray!"

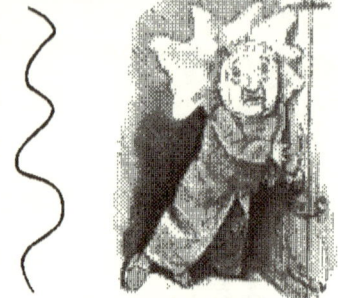

"Oh, I never had such a turn in my life!" he said.   "Fancy a lady in St. Stephen's!!!"

So he made haste to barricade the door with everything he could move.   But she missed a battering ram, and is sure to get in one day—and so she ought, poor thing!

OUR GRANDMOTHERLY M.P. ON COSTUME.

The Government has, we understand, is a burst of grandmotherliness, sent over our particular M.P. to Fiji, to suggest to the natives a few items in the way of additional clothing.

Now our M.P. is a quiet retiring man, and approached his subject with a—well, we might almost say—with dread. It wasn't that livelihood he minded—it was easy to button-hole them—(so to speak)—and make a few practical remarks ;

It was the LADIES. Here was the difficulty to a retiring though grandmotherly mind. However, he began well, by lending them a lot of umbrellas.

And, after all, what difficulty is insurmountable by perseverance and a slight knowledge of the sewing machine (ADVT.)? They really got on capitally after a time. In short—not to mince the matter—he says he'll be hanged if he comes back to England any more.

MORE ABOUT OUR M.P.

We learn that our Grandmotherly M.P. has received an intimation from the Government that his late refusal to return to his native land, when considered in connection with certain PAPAL EDICTS, seems to evince a desire on his part to throw off his CIVIL ALLEGIANCE.

Now, the fact is, our M.P. indignantly asserts that he had already embarked for England, and was sitting on the bowsprit, absorbed in the perusal of a very interesting treatise.

When he was suddenly carried off by a mermaid, and detained as a lunatic, on account of his headgear.

ON THE TRAIL
A DOMESTIC INCIDENT.

"There! If that cat ain't gone into the house with its muddy feet!" (*Enters.*)

"And all over the drawing-room, spoiling the carpet and the chairs!"

"Oh, dear! and all along the 'all and up the stairs. Just look at the footmarks!"

And the careful domestic followed up stairs to reprove that mischievous animal.

Then the master came home; and his eye fell upon the track; and he was seen to observe the most nobbly stick in the umbrella-stand and ascend the stairs. After that cat, no doubt.

OH, THAT MANCHESTER!

"Positively *terrible!*"—we were saying so to our laundress (a most intelligent, right-minded person) only the other day—"positively *terrible* to think of the rubbish they sell as lawn nowadays! Must be literally three-fourths 'dressing'—wears out *in our washing.*" Our laundress *entirely* agrees with our remarks:

She assures us that, after she has put one of our brand-new shirts in soak,

And in passing it through her patent "washer," is given her quite a turn to see *the amount of stuff that comes away*—all "dressing," of course.

And she's right enough, for our wife also remarks to us, "Is it not disgraceful? Here is the wash worn," and shows us a rag, or—a rag. Our laundress declares she's quite grieved by it—quite worn away. So are our shirts.

THE PENALTY OF FAME.

There was an Individual who yearned to be distinguished ;   And continually worshipped at the Temple of Fame.

And one fine day the Lady answered his summons ; but on the end of her skirts sat a BUGBEAR with an ADDRESS !
And the Fame Worshipper fled.

But Fame to him has a fine view, —and she caught him and held him while the BUGBEAR read him addresses until he lies in a prostrate state, little hoping being entertained of his recovery,

REVENGE IS SWEET.

1. "It's an ugly one," he thought, "and she knows it, and goes!"
2. "And remain in the forerunner of disrespect— my strokal will deprive her genius. She shall see see it."
3. So he attempted to hide it behind a picture.
4. But she would keep dusting that picture.
5. Then he arose in the night,—
6. And hid it beneath a mat.
7. But she would keep sweeping that mat.
8. Then he crept down to the kitchen,—
9. And in the dresser-drawer he found an ugly one of her.
10. It was his turn now.

THE BETRAYER

Such a Listener A. was! A great among listeners. First B. would invite him to dine, and detail to him minutely every uninteresting atom of his past life.

Then C. would invite him, and go right through those nine thousand and seventeen anecdotes of celebrities again.

And then D. would invite him, and recount his ten miles of "good things" he had said to fellows, or heard fellows say to fellows, or heard of fellows saying.

And one day, not content with *that*, the three together sent him an invite to dine, intending to have a right down good evening at him. There was a weird meaning in his face as he read the note.

He accepted. They sat at meat. *Then*, like a torrent, he burst forth—rattled off all B.'s past life right through—went on with C.'s nine anecdotes—encored D.'s ten miles of good things—and finally let 'em have the backs of twenty *Family Heralds*, five pages of the dictionary, and the winning numbers in the Paris Lottery. B., C., and D. *just* escaped being dead men,—but they tell no tales now.

THE IMPOSTOR.
THE TALE OF A SECRET ORGIE.

In society Browne was looked upon as a man of the most exalted æstheticism. He would tolerate no music but the ultra-hyper-incomprehensibility-tunsism.

He would gaze upon no picture except those by the queerest and most distorted masters.

And he had been known to fade into unconsciousness at the dinner-table on hearing onions spoken of . . . . .

And one day he was observed to shut up all the shutters and bolt all the doors in a most mysterious way.

And society peeped through a crack—and Browne, seated in a chamber hung with pictures by the most living artists, was consuming Irish stew, while his daughter played to him selections from Offenbach ! ! !

THE "POLITICAL" INCUBUS.

The "Political" haunted us through thick and thin; even popping his head out of a gun as we were about to load it, and saying :—"Oh, I was afraid you might be firing at the enemy, so I just got in here to prevent it."

Then he would say to the General, at a critical point of a battle :— "Better just let the enemy win this affair, and decimate our fellows —politically prudent, you know. Make a bath blunder; forget to support your attacking columns, or something." And the General generally (or un-), did make the blunder too.

What greatly surprised the "Political" was the friendliness of the natives to him. "Why, whenever I go among 'em they embrace me, and call me their dear friend !" he'd say.

THE DIFFICULTIES OF SOME GENERALS.

But just look at the difficulties some Generals have to contend with. Why, there's a General we know—(most intelligent fellow)—

Who only marched his troops straight on for a week, without any food—to be sure, the Department had forgotten to issue boots to them; but that was a mere trifle)—and the fellows were positively unable to fight for fatigue, and got beaten! What can a General do with such troops as that?

Then the officers! Why, that General left one officer alone with written orders to keep back the enemy—and he actually let himself be killed by them!

Then the enemy's ways were so underhanded. Why, they came upon him without any warning when he was having a quiet cigar, and not even thinking of them! No General could deal with enemies like that!

FROM SOUTH AFRICA AGAIN.

So *desperately* cunning those Zulu chiefs are! How can we expect to be awake to their stratagems? They sent a messenger to one of our officers to tell him there is such a pretty sight or such a nice heap of booty at such and such a spot, and no danger whatever. *How* is our officer to suspect anything wrong? He proceeds to that spot with a few troops.

Then, thousands of Zulus appear!—seem literally to spring up from the ground. Our officer hadn't observed the *least trace* of 'em before!—no more had his scouts! They *must* have been artfully hiding *behind their shields!*

There was a report about the other day that the War Office wanted a lot of fresh scouts for Zululand. There was a report that somebody saw the fellows we've sketched above waiting to present themselves as candidates for the service.

THE POLITICAL OFFENDER IN RUSSIA.

("AGE NO CONSIDERATION.")

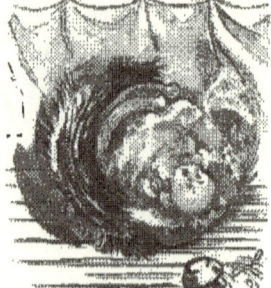

The police had long suspected him of some connection with a notorious "Ring."

Indeed he had been observed to evince Revolutionary Inclinations;

And one day it came to light that he had a finger in the Most Dangerous Portion of the Press;

While there was no doubt as to his indulging in Subversive Designs.

In view of all this the Emperor had but one alternative—Siberia.

AN UNPRECEDENTED LARK.

"Such a lark we 'ad—me an' Tom an' 'Arry! Wouldn't come off the hice when it wos a-givin' way, an' dodged the police all over the shop."

"Such a lark! We all tumbled him, we did, an' 'ad a reg'lar crowd a-riskin' their lives to save ours!"

"Such a lark! I went an' 'ad rheumatic fever; an' Tom went an' 'ad a shock to his system; and neether of us ain't right yet, and ain't never likely to be agin! And as to 'Arry, there was a inquest on 'em and another on the 'Umane Society cove as tried to save 'im. Such a lark!"

"A powerful stroke."

"A well-built 'Cheque.'"

"Well pulled through."

"Choice of Stations."

"Feeling his stretcher."

"A rapid recovery."

OUR GAS

He had just had the gas laid on. "Now," he said, "I'll sit down and have such a read by my new gas!"

As the hour flew by, he might have been observed to become gradually covered with a thin coating of sulphur.

More time flew by; the coating increased in thickness.

Anxious friends called, and looked for him in vain.

It was some centuries later (observe, by the way, the style of dress, somewhat resembling a diver's, in vogue in England at that future period) when Guy found a human form strangely preserved in a coating of sulphur, and placed it in a museum.

This is really the extract of the excrusted forms unearthed at Pompeii; they burned gas, supplied by a company similar to ours!

OUR BENEFIT SOCIETY.

We had a beautiful back Benefit Society, and, as we was all pretty strong and hearty, and never ill, we used to have a nice little convivial "sing-song" evening (twice a week with the hands.

When, one day, an Old Boy joined the society. That Old Boy had "such fun" written all over him.

Well, he got ill there and then, and, if you'll believe it, he stuck at it regular. There he'd sit, enjoyin' gallon after gallon o' medium and drawing his fellow shilling a week sick-pay. We'd 'ad to keep 'im—we couldn't get rid; we'd only got to pay up our shilling a week.

Well, we got to that pitch we couldn't stand it no longer; so we all made a desprit effort and went ill. And that Old Boy was pronounced cured, and—he I he I—couldn't git ill no more; so he just 'ad to keep the lot on us—and a sight of medium we got through too—oh, no !

A QUESTION OF TITLE.

They were a very serious family. Sunday was their only opportunity for reading. There was a deliciously questionable story in a magazine—a story they pined to read. But the magazine was called the "Workaday World; a Magazine of Amusement"—and they couldn't think of reading a magazine of that secular title on Sunday.

So they went inconsiderately to the Editor and wheedled him to change the title of the mag. And the Editor, being a shrewd man,—

Altered it to "The Sabbath Crook and Sheep-Pen; a Magazine of Earnest Reflection." Then they read that deliciously questionable story, "Divorce or Rescue?" with devotional relish.

FURTHER SUNDAY READING.

There was another deliciously questionable story in the book-case which he longed to read on Sunday, but he couldn't get the earlier side of the book abuved *his* taste, and he could not, of course, think of reading it under these circumstances. . . .

At this time he remembered a poor relation whom it would only be charity to ask to dinner on Sunday, and who loved reading, and had a habit (being deaf) of reading to himself ALOUD; so he invited the poor relation,—

Who came, and enjoyed the dinner very much;

Then, when he had his pipe and glass, his host placed before him that tempting secularly-read volume;

And the poor relation soon got enjoyably absorbed in it; and the only hitch was that he had lost his habit of reading to himself ALOUD.

"My dear," said his host, after he had left that night, "I shall NOT invite him again, for I cannot but disapprove of his unbecoming choice of literature for perusal on the Sabbath."

TURFISM TURNED TOPSY-TURVY.

OUR NATIONAL FAULT.

We are a sad, unsociable nation, we English. We do not go out enough—we are too fond of home!

Why do we not open cheerful cafés, now, and sit gaily outside them, enjoying the fresh air and the harmless glass?

Then, the simpler forms of music are not common enough among us—we neglect them cruelly! Even under their influence we are sad;
What a dull nation!

THE CRUSHING 'BUS-DRIVER.

You are drawn, fascinated, to the 'Bus-driver by the immovable air of mystic profundity in his still, wise eyes. Your air by him is new; and feel that your premiere ambition is to make him smile and notice you. You try, try, try to find some remark which will not be met by his silent scorn or his cold derision.

You make a remark. Five minutes glide by, then he leans over and looks at you. You shrink.

Ten more minutes go. He slowly commences to chuckle.

After this he seems to point you out to himself for his own derision.

BEAUTIFUL EXAMPLE OF COMPUNCTION.

*"A cabman, who said he * * succumbed to temptation in consequence of the weather (on Whit Monday), was fined 12s. for being drunk whilst in charge of his horse and cab."—MR. NEWSPAPER.*

He could not bear that his business should be so flourishing at the price of dampness and misery to his fellow-men. He was filled with misery; his earnings were enormous.

He shrank from the cab, and bought an umbrella and mackintosh business. Still he flourished out of the wetness and grief of his fellows. His heart sank; he was becoming affluent.

He could bear it no longer. He invested his fortune in a straw umbrellas, sunshade, pith-helmet and parasol trade. No purchasers came now; his stock rotted; he sank to rags and beggary; his conscience was at ease; he had found happiness at last!

THE MYSTERIOUS ATTRACTION.

AS SHADOWED FORTH BY THE ARGUMENTS AGAINST THE DECEASED WIFE'S SISTER BILL.

There were women handsomer than she, yet he felt, from the first moment of seeing her, that she exercised an irresistible fascination over him.

"What can it mean, this strange yearning?" he mused; "something tells me that we are intended for each other — and yet, my present wife——!"

But she knew the secret of it! She grasped the wrist of his wife. "I am because I am your sister-r-r-r—his wife's sister-r-r-r!" she hissed.

Indeed, she felt that he was to be hers; and she refused a King and two Dukes—and waited.

ECCENTRICITIES OF THE ELECTRIC CURRENT.

Having a suspicion that the electric current is—whether owing to meteorological influences or to "irresponsibility"—no longer so reliable as it was once supposed to be, Jones, an eminent member of the Public, made an interesting experiment the other day with a view to throwing light on the subject. Having arranged that his father should be in immediate need of medical help, Jones commenced the interesting experiment by attempting to send a telegram from the nearest post-office to the physician. We give result of experiment:—

Slight diversion of the electric current for a time, to begin with;

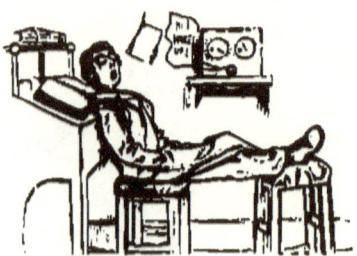

Trifling suspension of the current at post office;

Singular interruption of the current for a few hours, further on. Meanwhile Jones's old relative expired. However, "The Department is not liable for losses incurred through the incorrect transmission, delay, or non-delivery of telegrams." (!)

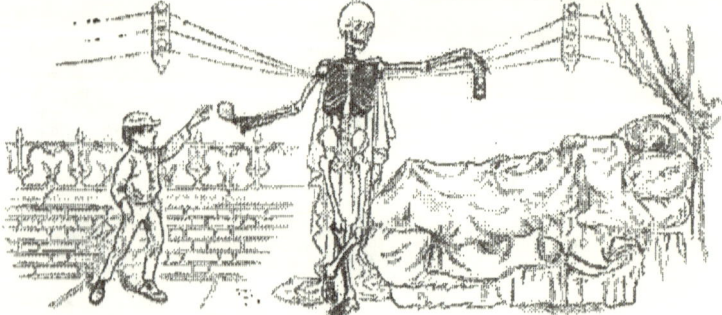

THE BOOK BORROWER.

You never mind lending your most cherished books to him, for he always is so careful to cover them. Yes, you lend him the book he asks for, on the understanding that he doesn't undervalue it; then,—

"Well, old fellow," he says to a friend, "I said I would not lend this to anybody, but I might just lend it to you, if you'll promise not to let it go out of your hands."

"What!" says that friend to his son, "lend you this book to paint the pictures"? Well, I said I'd—but I suppose there's no harm in lending it to you."

"I've got you that book," says that son to his schoolfellow; "but you mustn't lend it to anybody else, nor cut out any of the pictures."

"Dear, dear!" exclaims the original borrower, when he gets the book back a year later, "it certainly isn't so fresh as it was! It's really time I covered it to prevent its getting damaged."

And then he brings it back so neatly wrapped in brown paper that you hardly scarcely worse to him, and you lend him a priceless MS.—and his little friends make drumheads of it.

BOOKS AGAIN.

There was a Book-Fancier who, resolved on an intellectual history treat, got a most valuable work,—

And got his daughter to read it to him. "A most suitingly written and improving work—most enjoyable!" he said.

And there was another Book-Fancier who was jealous of the first one's possession of that valuable work, and grieved in and saw his enjoyment,—

And went to his study and hatched a vengeful scheme to spoil that first one's delight.

Then he burst in upon him, and confidentially assured him that the volume was not a GENUINE FIRST EDITION; and the first Book-Fancier beat his breast, and asked his daughter how she dared read such illiterate trash to HIM! For impostures and I's for i's are hateness; and good type and white paper are an abomination unto them that know.

"TO SUIT ALL CUSTOMERS."

"*Want a waterproof coat, sir?* Yes. We keep them at all prices. *Wish for a cheap one, sir?* Certainly—you may place entire confidence in our very cheapest articles; we keep nothing bad."

"*You think you'd prefer one at a medium price, sir?* I should recommend that too; you see, these cheapest ones are apt to come to bits at the least pull—couldn't recommend them."

"*Like a better one still, sir?* Well, I think you are wise. You see, you can stick your fingers through these medium-priced ones when they get wet."

THE RIGHT PRINCIPLE.

You cannot see around noticing the thoroughness and conscientiousness of the work in Dabb's picture. Every detail pushed down to the ear of Indian elephant and the nursery pin; the figures are of minor importance.

That one for instance. He travelled all the way to India to draw it under the right circumstances, taking the car with him in case he should find none there.

Then there's the fine weather-stained face of the principal figure, browned in Afric's sun. Took his model to Africa, and made him sit while he watched him brown for three months.

Then he wanted to get the true aspect of a corkscrew on the track of a mast in a gale. And he went up and drew it there too.

But when he wanted to watch the effect on cast bottom of the moment of the wearer's being blown up by a shell, the model raised obstacles.

So the picture was spoilt by this one point, and Dabb was never happy about it.

He was such a hopeful little gentleman! He laid in a beautiful watering-pot and lovely hose. Then was late Winter; it rained; but he looked out of the window and thought:—"It will clear up presently, and then I will garden."

The Spring came; it rained; but rain is good in the Spring; he went out and watered.

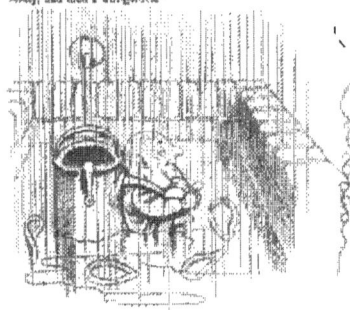

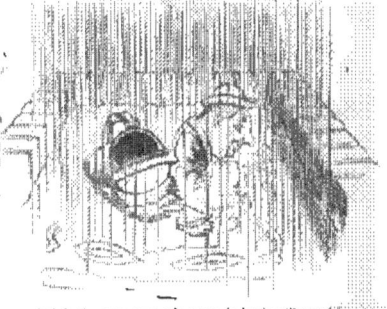

The Summer began; it rained; but he sat in his garden to watch for the flowers coming up, and said:—"It will clear up by-and-by, and then I will go in-doors and hope."

And the Summer progressed; it rained; but he still peered down to see the flowers come up.

And the Autumn came; it rained; yet he floated about (still hoping) and watched for the flowers.

And at length (while it rained) the flowers did come; and the enthusiast triumphed. They were not the flowers he had expected; but no doubt he had mixed up the seeds.

THE COMPLETE BUILDER-LANDLORD.
(BY ONE WHO HAS BEEN A TENANT.)
No. 1.—ON CHOICE OF SITE AND FOUNDATIONS.

There are many practical jokes ready for you to indulge in, O Speculative Builder-Landlord! So plentiful are they that above all other mortals. Here is one.—Choose a nice damp pudding clay for a site, and order in a lot of stock-baked bricks.

Then "put up" a pair of villas of the modern composite-incomprehensible order.

Then get two parties peculiarly resentful of any disturbance of their privacy,

And get them comfortably settled as Tenants in your villas.

No. 2.—THE MUD WALL CONCEIT.

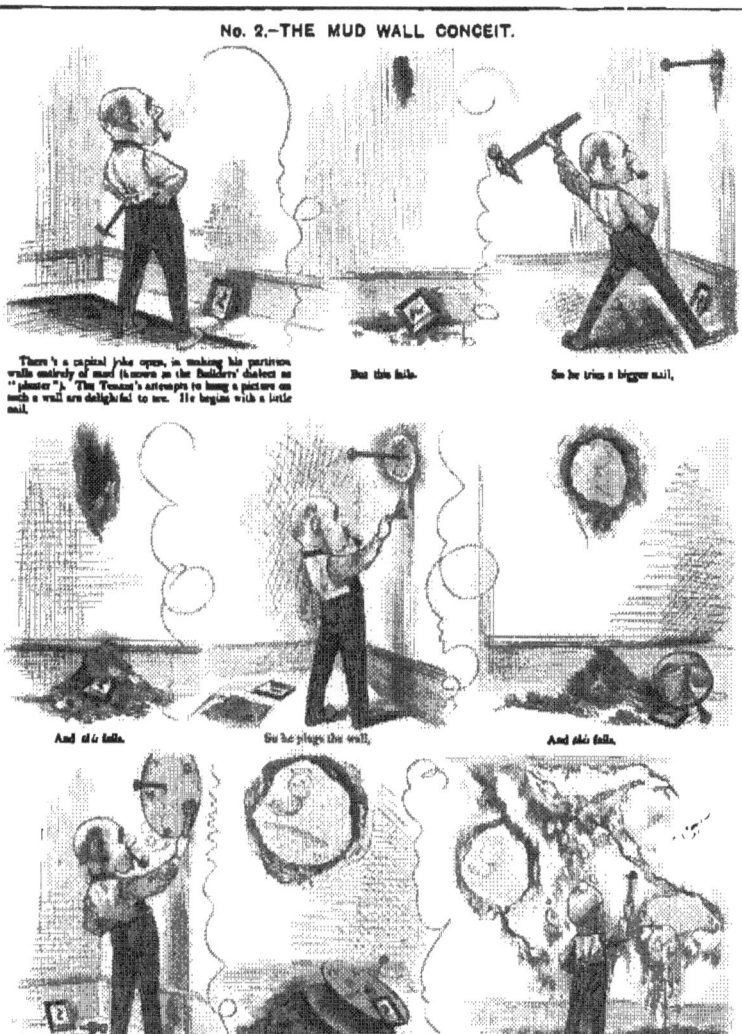

There 's a capital joke open, in making his partition walls entirely of mud (known in the Builders' dialect as "plaster"). The Tenant's attempts to hang a picture on such a wall are delightful to see. He begins with a little nail.

But this fails.

So he tries a bigger nail,

And this fails.

So he plugs the wall,

And this fails.

So he puts a plate on each side of the wall,

And still fails.

Then he taps lightly along the wall to find a firmer place, and

No. 3.—PREPARING A GARDEN.

Experience sooner or a present at the mind the delight that you, Mr. Speculative Builder, feel in preparing the "gardens" attached to your house.
This is simply done by burying all the hard building refuse all over them.

"*Nice little garden,*" says the Tenant; "I'll just plant a few
things in it, and turn up the earth a bit."

And then to remark his emotions as he does turn up the earth a bit!

And to see him just passing the lawn-mower over the grass!

At length he fancies he might get on a bit better by removing the brickbats and things; then you, Mr. Builder-Landlord, drop in: "Ah, removing
the earth," you say; "mind, I shall expect you to replace it when you leave." And the joy of the Tenant!

No. 4.—THE CISTERN LARK.

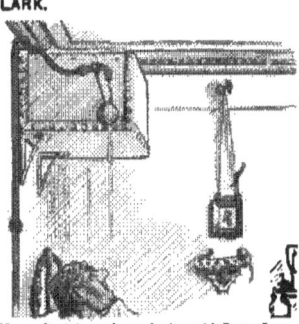

"Great fun to be got out of a cistern! Is building. Mr. Builder never designs a suitable place for it; then you find that the only possible place for it is in the best bed-room. "Unsightly!!!" you say to the Tenant; "why, it takes away from the bareness of the walls, and here it won't be exposed to frosts in the winter."

Don't fasten the supply-pipe and ball-tap. Leave it to wave about. In a short time it will just pump over the edge of the cistern to have a look round.

Then, when the Tenant complains, fasten it to the ceiling; ball-taps always attend well or stick fast; but it will send little spurts all over the ceiling;

Then, when the Tenant complains again, screw it tighter. Then it will suck and overflow.

"Don't you think those supports look like giving way?" says the Tenant. "Well," you reply, "they might be braver for a coat of paint."

But they aren't. Then it is a goes!

No. 5.—WAYS AND PASSAGES.

Always make the very most of your ground; leave no side entrance.
"'Ere's the dustman," says the servant to the Tenant.

"Great Universe!" says the Tenant, "there is no side entrance for him."

So first of all he gets the dustman to come along the wall from the end of the road.

Then he tries getting him over the top of the house.

But at length these little arrangements become somewhat tedious. "There!!!" gasps the Tenant, "let him come through the drawing-room—and the coals too—and everything else!"

No. 6.—STAIRCASES.

4. Until that Guest sticks in a narrow gorge, never to extricate again.

2. Up goes the Guest. For the first flight all is safe and easy;

1. Such pleasantry to be had out of staircases, too! "Good night, old boy," sobs the Tenant to his Guest. "Mind the stairs; may you come down again!"

5. As for the servant, her easiest way is to swing herself on a rope down to the kitchen, tray and all. She may alight mildly thus.

No. 7.—BOLTS AND BARS.

And then your bolts and things. An inexhaustible source of fun. "Bolts!" says the Ironmonger to whom you go; "yes; something of this sort."

"No," you say; "I'm a *Builder*." "Oh, ah!" says the Ironmonger. "Something of *this* sort! Fifty in the ounce."

Then the Tenant's first care, on entering into tenancy, is to see that all the shutters have been provided with bolts.

"Be very careful," he says impressively to his servant, "that you bolt every bolt at night. Then we are safe."

"Yes," he murmurs to himself, "one can sleep with confidence when one knows that all the bolts are returned."

"There! What a start these 'ere shutters do give yer. I just put my finger agin it, and down it went and give me quite a turn!"

No. 8.—THE DOOR-HANDLE SPREE.

Oh, and door-handles, too ! You say to your general Plumber-Carpenter-Painter-Labourer-and-Man-of-all-work. "Here are the handles ; but mind you don't put them on till the day before the Tenant enters, as they aren't warranted to bear more than a week's wear."

So the Tenant having entered, asks a friend to look at his new house. "Come to, old fellow," says he, "I'll show you the rooms."

"Hullo !" says he, "here 's the handle off the drawing-room door ; so we can't get in there."

"Why, here 's the bed-room door-handle off, too ! Can't go in there. I 'll just pocket all the handles that come off, and show 'em to the Landlord !" And he pockets a good pocketful.

"I 'm afraid we must have a quiet smoke on the stairs, old boy."

"Well, good bye," he says ; "sorry you couldn't see the rooms ;

No. 9.—THE DRAINS AND DUSTHOLE WITTICISM.

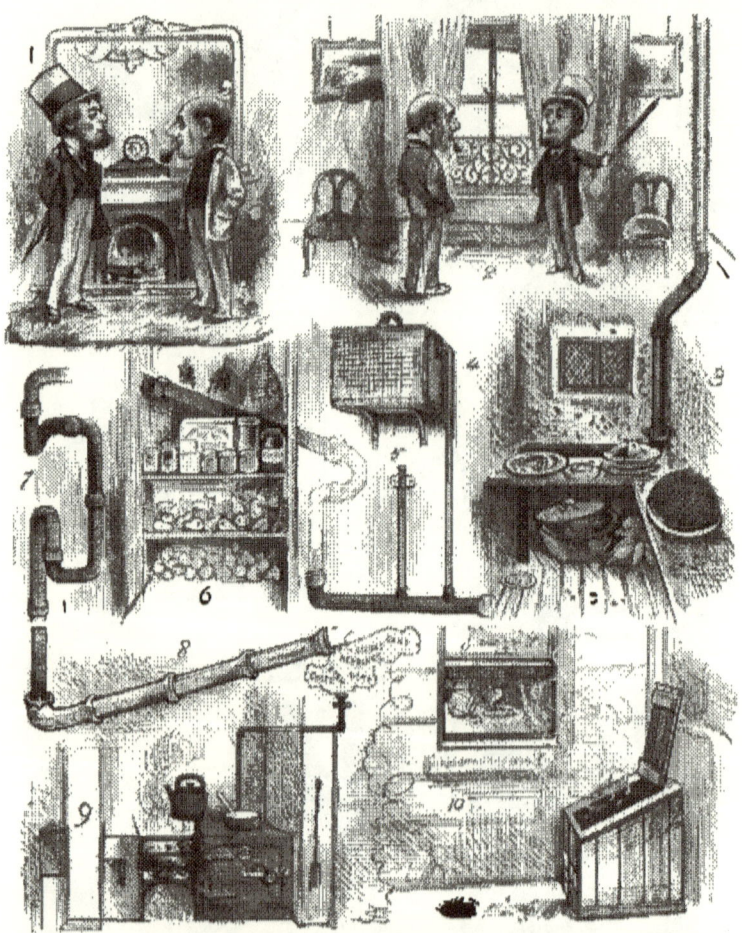

1 "Now," says the Tenant, "tell me how you've arranged the drain-pipes ; I always like to know where to find 'em." 2. "Oh, first-class drainage !" you reply. "First of all, you see, I've brought the pipes down a corner of the dining-room ; (3) then through the pantry, where there's a ventilating trap ; (4) then there's the waste-pipe, which ventilates the drains into the cistern, (5) and another pipe ventilating 'em into the breakfast-room ; (6) then the drains run through a store cupboard ; (7) then they bend up and down a bit ; (8) and finally slant upwards, with all the joints the wrong way, to the main drain. 9. Then I've ventilated the oven into the drawing-room, which'll help to warm the room tremendously ; (10) and I've put your dusthole close under the breakfast-room."

www.ingramcontent.com/pod-product-compliance
Lightning Source LLC
Chambersburg PA
CBHW021227020726
47498CB00008B/2727